Long Time Ago Good

Long Time Ago Good

Stories

Lowell Mick White

Buffalo Times Press
AUSTIN

The characters and events in this book are fictitious. Any resemblance to actual persons, living or dead, is coincidental.

Grateful acknowledgment is made to the following publications, where some of these stories were first published:

Callaloo: "Five Things"
Iron Horse Literary Review: "The Speed of Sound"
Short Story: "Reliction"
Mosaic Mind: "Bad Guts"
Southwestern American Literature: "Wildlife Rehabilitation"

Cover Photograph: Marc St. Gil, US National Archives and Records Administration
Author Photograph: Reji Thomas
Book Design: Buffalo Time Productions

Library of Congress Cataloging-in-Publication Data

White, Lowell Mick, 1958-

Long time ago good : stories / Lowell Mick White.

ISBN-10: 0-9908632-8-X
ISBN-13: 978-0-9908632-8-1

p. cm.

I. Title.

PS3623.H57865L66 2009

813'.6--dc22 2008035240

For Patricia Bjorklund

Acknowledgments

Lots of people helped in lots of ways, and their help is deeply appreciated: Pamela Booton, Abigail Bowers, Alan Gingras, Bea Gyimah, James Hannah, Alysa Hayes, Rachel Strecker Nikolaiev, Marco Portales, Chuck Taylor.

Several of these stories were written while I held the Dobie-Paisano Fellowship. Thanks goes to the Texas Institute of Letters and the University of Texas at Austin for the fellowship—and, of course, to Dr. Audrey Slate, for all her many kindnesses.

The great pain in our heart we are
now trying to alleviate by following the
mirages of new frontiers. On the broad
flat plain of monotonous living we see
the distorted images of our desires
glimmering on the horizons of the future;
we press on toward them only to have
them disappear completely or reappear in
different form in another direction.

—Walter Prescott Webb

Long time ago good. Now not so good.

—Hemingway

Long Time Ago Good

Top Dog in the Kill Chain

After she moved to Texas from California, Marla Hayden decided she needed some Western Art on her wall. She found a Charlie Russell print online and bought it—a painting of a haggard, miserable, freezing steer caught out in the middle of a blizzard, surrounded by hungry wolves. It was called "Waiting for a Chinook," a Chinook being a warmer wind that would sometimes blow across the Northern Plains for a few winter days. Marla had the print professionally framed and she hung it over the couch in her living room. Though she liked the cool, soothing blues and grays of the painting, she mostly liked it because she saw herself as one of the wolves—an alpha bitch, perhaps, successful and fearless. But when the software company she worked for, Nntych, laid off 300 people, including her fiancé, who worked in the finance department, and shipped another 150 or so jobs to India, Marla took the print down and put it in the back of the utility room and hung drying clothes off the edge of the frame. Maybe she wasn't a wolf, after all. Six months later her boss told her, very casually, that her own job was also going to Bangalore.

The next day Marla called in sick.

For most of the morning she lay on the couch watching television, gazing solemnly at a series of bad comics on the comedy channel. She hadn't had the heart to tell her fiancé, Jim Lueckert, about her job the night before. He had been telling her for months that her job was in danger—even before his own layoff he had been telling her that Nntych was in trouble, that sales were lagging, that the officers had been spending far too much money. But that seemed absurd: even after the great boom of the late nineties it was apparent that growth, slower growth, sure, but growth would go on forever, forever, everybody knew it, you only had to look around Austin. Seventy or so people a day were still moving in—the streets were jammed, new housing developments were going up everywhere, new strip malls, new buildings downtown, in the three years she had lived in Austin the city had been transformed—it was a totally different place, and was still changing, still becoming. And Nntych was a strong young company, an innovator, Nntych hired the smartest kids from the best colleges in the country and they were putting out the best systems management software in the world. Nothing could stop them.

Her cell phone rang. Marla glanced at the displayed number—it was Jim, calling from his new job. She punched the button to answer.

"Hi," she said.

"I called you at work," Jim said. "They said you were sick."

"Yeah, they were right."

"Marla—"

"Oh, it's nothing," Marla said. "I'm just tired—my stomach's messed up, too. I just figured I'd take the day off."

"Poor baby," Jim said. "You want me to bring you something?"

Marla looked at the wall where Charlie Russell's doomed steer had been. Where the successful, hardy wolves had been. In its place she had put up a corny painting of Texas bluebonnets, a horrible painting of a happy dog romping in an endless field of cheerful blue flowers in the spring sunshine, a painting so ugly and bad it was actually kind of cool. If you had a sense of humor and were maybe colorblind, too.

"No," Marla said. "Maybe later—I think I'll go back to sleep."

Jim worked in the billing office of a large law firm downtown and considered himself lucky to have found a decent job. Where was she going to go? Who wanted programmers anymore? Who wanted front-line managers anymore? India was taking all the jobs—everybody over there in India was a genius, and they worked for nothing. It wasn't fair. Marla dreaded having to break down and tell Jim that he had been right about Nntych the whole time.

Fucking Nntych! Goddamn corporate culture! Greed, idiocy, short-sighted foolishness! The big managers had ruined everything. Jim had told her that the canceling of the cab perk had been the first outward sign that the company was in trouble. The cab perk: Nntych's recruitment brochures talked about the company's "work hard, play hard" philosophy, but the company also frowned on drunk driving and so had offered free cab rides—unlimited free cab rides—to all employees. Jim told her the cab perk cost the company almost $30,000 a month. Really, they all took cabs all the time, everyone, all the employees, all the young people from the best colleges in the country, all of them new to Austin, new to Texas, new to each other, taking cabs down to the Sixth Street nightclub area two, three, four times a week, maybe stopping to get sushi on the way downtown, then milling with the vast crowds along the street, partying along with students from the university, other high tech workers, some locals, everyone drinking and laughing. On some corners, mostly toward the east end of Sixth, there would be knots of hard-looking young black men and they always sort of shocked Marla: they scared Marla, though she knew she wasn't racist—California had lots of black people, of course, and lots of Mexicans and Asians, too, Marla got along with everyone, she treated everyone the same—but these young men, they scared her with their open shirts and flat rippling bellies, and they disturbed her because they weren't supposed to be there. Texas wasn't black people—Texas was cowboys. Texas was George Bush. Texas was the old frontier, where stupid white guys in pickup trucks would drive around and drink beer and brag about barbeque or football or something equally vulgar.

In a group with Jim and their friends from work, Marla would sometimes circle Sixth Street in the bright flickering neon night, shot bar to shot bar to dance club and on and on, and she felt safe in her group, even though when a hard young black man might try to get their attention—"Hey, can you tell me what time it is?"—no one would answer, they would fall silent, and they would all keep walking silently until they crossed the street and went up the block or whatever. Generally, Marla and her friends kept to the west end of the street; it seemed safer, and the bars were just as fun. Later, going home in the free cabs, taking long trips to their homes in the far Southwest or far Northwest sides of town, everyone would be laughing and making calls on their cell phones, gossiping about work, telling each other how wonderful Austin was, with restaurants and Sixth Street and music and all the cool people at work, but how weird and crude and out of it the rest of Texas was—Texas they had seen only from car windows as they drove in from San Diego or wherever, or gazed down on from a mile up in the air as they flew in from Seattle or Boston—and the cab would speed by neighborhoods where the locals lived, the ones they saw on the TV news for winning chili cook-offs, or going on killing sprees, or getting in car wrecks, all those would-be cowboys sitting in the night in their camped little houses drinking beer and cleaning their guns and admiring their Confederate flags while their girlfriends snorted crank and their kids rolled around squalling in dirty diapers—a whole class of left-behind losers that no one would ever take seriously. The cab driver if he was cool would laugh along with them, knowing he was getting a good fare and a good tip, and it had all been such childlike, endless fun, one long party, it was never going to stop, the jobs would get better and better, and pay more and more and more—but, no, now it *had* ended. It had stopped.

The idiots who ran Nntych had totally screwed everything up. They cut the cab perk, and that was the first sign the company was in trouble. Then they downsized, and downsized again. They still made money and the stock went up, so they went ahead and outsourced. Marla wondered, What did those fuckers over in India need *her* job for? She had house payments to make.

After she told Jim to call her back later, Marla rolled to her side and found herself gazing into the eyes of Ginger, a sleek long-haired dachshund. She scooped Ginger up onto the couch and hugged her tight.

"Oh, baby," she whispered, "what're we gonna do?"

Ginger didn't say anything and snuggled up close to her and they drifted off to sleep.

★ ★ ★

When Marla awoke she saw from the clock on the DVD player that she had slept some three hours. It was early afternoon. She'd placed the TV on mute when Jim called; it was still on, showing a movie or something with a car racing around banging into things. Ginger was scratching at the patio door to get out. Marla found the remote and switched the TV over to a news show, where people were screaming at each other about something. She didn't want to know what; she kept the television muted. She got up and let Ginger out into the back yard, and went to pull a Diet Dr. Pepper from the refrigerator. Then she heard angry barking coming from outside.

"Baby!" she yelled.

Marla dropped the Dr. Pepper on the kitchen counter and went to the door. Ginger was at the edge of the yard, frozen, staring at the privacy fence. Barking was coming from the other side of the fence; a nasty brindled pit bull lived over there.

"Ginger! Get in here!"

Ginger didn't move—growling, maybe. The barking and snarling—more than one dog, Marla could tell—went on.

"Ginger!"

Marla went out and crossed the yard in her bare feet. The afternoon was hot: even the grass felt hot, and the peonies planted along the back of the fence were wilting under the gray hazy sky. The barking beyond the fence was growing—snarling, growling. Ginger's teeth were bared and she stood trembling staring at the fence until Marla yanked her up and held her tight.

There was movement on the other side of the fence—a dog fight. Marla stepped over to peer through a knothole but a giant pale shape—a dog?—slammed into the fence and she jumped back. Ginger was wriggling in her arms.

"Hey!"

The dog on the other side of the fence sounded like it was trying to chew through the fence—to attack her, to get Ginger. Then it sounded like there was another dog over there—and maybe another. The anger radiating through the wooden fence was incredible. Marla took another step back. Ginger was growling.

"Be quiet," Marla said. Ginger struggled to get down out of her arms and so Marla turned and went back to the house and dropped Ginger inside. The little dog tried to shoot out but Marla blocked her with a leg and slid the patio door shut. Ginger looked up at her through the glass.

The dog noise from next door grew—two or three dogs—a dog fight. Marla slowly crossed the lawn and stood next to the fence. It was shaking. Marla placed her hand on the rough wood: she could feel the vibrations of snaps and growls transformed, not just hearing them now, but feeling them. She looked through the knothole: nothing. Marla put her foot on the bottom of the fence and pulled herself to the top and looked over. She saw two big dogs, strange dogs, a white one and a brown one, savaging the brindled pit.

"Stop it!" she yelled. "Hey!"

The brindled pit was in a corner trying to protect itself.

The two other dogs—also pits, Marla saw, big ones—were going after the brindled dog, the brown one at its flanks, the pale one going for the throat.

"Stop it!"

The dogs ignored her. Marla dropped down from the fence and ran to the gate at the edge of her backyard. It was locked. The fighting dogs sounded like they were going crazy. Marla crossed to the patio and went inside the house—pushing Ginger out of the way—through the living room and out the front door. She ran next to the house next door and rang the bell. There was no answer, so she banged on the door with her fist and yelled. The house was dark—she was pretty sure the people were away. She didn't know their names, had only seen them occasionally, brown-skinned people from Pakistan or Mexico or someplace, people who wore nice clothes, had a nice Mitsubishi and a big Ford Excursion. They had that brindled pit bull, too. But a lot of people had big dogs, sometimes when Jim went running in the neighborhood rather than down by the lake, Marla could tell what block he was on by where the dogs were barking at him—though now, someone's big dogs were loose and had gone after the brindled dog—they could have gone after a child, if there had been children in the neighborhood, or if one had been on the street.

Marla looked around. All the houses on the block were blank-looking, closed off, with small windows on the front and recessed doors, big houses of stone or brick that almost filled their lots and seemed to push forward with seven-foot wooden privacy fences crowding up behind them. It was a good, new neighborhood, people had to have good jobs to live out on the far edge of town with their cars and big dogs, and apparently everyone was off at their jobs now, for nothing was moving.

The dogs were still fighting. Marla ran back to her own house and went inside. Ginger was waiting for her by the front door. "Stay!" Marla said as she crossed the house and went out the back, but Ginger followed her through the house to the sliding patio doors and stood and watched. Marla went to the side of the house and began pulling at the water hose—she'd maybe spray water at the dogs, get them all wet and make them stop—when there was a quick pause in the dog noise from next door. Then a growl, a snap, and then silence.

Marla dropped the hose and went over to the fence and listened. She thought she might be hearing the panting of tired dogs. She pulled herself to the top of the fence and saw the brindled dog dying, sprawled out in the sun, bleeding, trailing guts, a hind leg twitching. The brown dog and the creamy one were in the shade next to the house, resting, panting, pink tongues lolling, looking over at her. The creamy one had what looked like blood on its face and neck. Marla watched the dogs for a long time before she dropped off the fence and went back inside her home.

★ ★ ★

In the evening, after work, Jim came over and let himself in. He brought her a bottle of wine, and cans of chicken soup, and a couple of movies to watch. Marla was still drowsy—disturbed—as he was unpacking, getting herself a glass of water, and she almost didn't notice when Jim stepped over and opened the patio door to let Ginger out.

"No!" Marla jumped over and slammed the door shut, almost catching Ginger in it. "No!" she said. "Ginger only goes out with a leash now—only with a leash."

"Baby?" Jim asked slowly. "Are you okay?"

"Fuck no, I'm not okay," Marla said. She pulled Ginger's leash down from a hook and fastened it to the squirming dog's collar. She noticed her hands were shaking, and she frowned up at Jim. "Don't just stare at me—go fix some soup or something."

Outside the evening was quiet and warm. Car sounds came from the distant expressway. Marla walked Ginger past the yard's sole tree, a lonely mesquite, tugging Ginger at times, the stubborn small dog not used to a leash in her own back yard. Then Marla went back and tied the leash to the tree. Marla left Ginger and touched the fence. The wood was warm and motionless. No sound came from beyond it. Marla pulled herself up and looked over the top.

She saw a black lump in the center of the yard, a dark lump close to where she had last seen the dead brindled pit. There was no sign of the cream-colored dog or the brown one. She was sure they were gone. The house beyond was dark. All the other houses in the neighborhood were dark. Nothing moved.

"Marla?" It was Jim, standing out on her patio. "Marla? Are you okay? Is something wrong?"

Everything's wrong, Marla thought. But she didn't say anything. She swung over the fence and came down into the back yard next door. The dead pit was in front of her, a few feet away, and in the dark it seemed to move. Marla took a step toward it. She could hear Jim calling, "Marla! Marla!" and even though he sounded like he was just on the other side of the fence, she didn't answer. She heard Jim say, "Ginger, what's wrong with your mommy?" Marla focused on the dark dog stretched out on the ground—maybe it moved again. Then it *did* move—it wasn't dead. The hind leg sort of kicked or scratched or something, and Marla knelt down beside the dog, and she touched its shoulder and said, "Poor boy." Then the brindled pit wrenched around and snapped her by the wrist.

★ ★ ★

The next afternoon Marla went to work. Nntych's headquarters were in an office park located on top of a canyon on the far west side of town, and from the parking lot Marla could look down at the flooded river below, Lake Austin, and the Loop 360 Bridge crossing it, and beyond the bridge to the towers of the city. There were two boats down below her on the lake towing water-skiers, and a few golfers strolled around at the country club course just downstream from the bridge. People at play under the hot white Texas sun, she thought, Texans at play, and the thought made her angry. The play seemed just a gloss over something incredibly crude and vulgar. Above her vultures rose floating on the updraft from the water, while grackles strutted around the parking lot picking at bits of trash.

She turned her back on them and went inside. Marla passed the security desk and the silent, newspaper-reading guard and took an elevator up to the third floor. She walked down a long, open room, passing several empty, sterile, office cubicles, and other cubicles occupied by bored or depressed-looking people, cubicles that were soon to be empty. Her boss, Conrad, was standing outside his office door—he had a real office instead of a cubicle, an office with a door and a window—and he saw the bandage on her forearm and asked, "Are you all right?" but she walked past him, like a zombie, and took her chair, at her desk. Some weeks before Jim had given her a half-dozen little plastic frogs to put on her desk, to cheer the place up, and three days earlier, in a playful mood, Marla had arranged the frogs in a long, humping daisy-chain of sexual frolic. Now, though, Marla just looked at the happy frogs and sighed and said, "Well, shit."

Bad Guts

Stranded and carless, victim of a lucky flat tire that kept him from going to work, newspaper columnist Wes Leonard sat in a dark bar, drinking beer after beer and thinking about the dangers of the world. If he leaned back a bit on his stool, he could see out through the thick glass of the door, see the street in front of the tavern, see a pothole in the street. Traffic was roaring along, a blur, and every now and then a car's tire would hit the pothole with a solid *thunk*—a dangerous, hollow sound that he could feel deep in his chest, a sound he knew represented the danger of blow-outs and lost lives. There was danger on the streets, he thought. Danger everywhere. Danger—maybe he could turn that into a story.

Jillian the barmaid came over to him. She asked, "Want another?"

"Sure," Wes said. He dug around in his change pile and pushed some money over to Jillian. She took his pitcher over to the tap to fill it. Wes said, "You know, I bet if we sat here long enough, somebody would drive over that hole and blow out a tire. Eventually everybody in town would drive over that hole and get a flat tire."

"You sound pretty happy about that," Jillian said. She sat the pitcher of beer down in front of him.

"Sure," Wes said. "Then nobody'd have to go to work."

"People would sit at home and starve," Jillian said. "You just want to share the misery."

Wes looked at Jillian. "That's an excellent idea." He flipped open his slim reporter's notebook and wrote SHARE THE MISERY. "Maybe I can do something with that."

Wes sipped his beer and watched as Jillian turned the notebook around and scratched out SHARE THE MISERY. Then she crossed out DANGER EVERYWHERE and put a little frowny face by it:

:(

Then she tapped on a word he had written at the top of the page: GUTS.

"Guts?" Jillian asked. She arched an eyebrow. "Just—guts?"

"Just guts," Wes repeated. He poured more beer into his mug.

"I see," Jillian said. She sat back down on a beer box and looked up at the television. Men were playing golf.

"*Bad* guts," Wes said.

Jillian looked back at him and blinked. "Oh, of course," she said. "Bad guts. I haven't seen any good guts around here in a long time."

"No," Wes said. "I'm serious. These are bad guts. I was supposed to go out to Pflugerville this afternoon to be the celebrity judge at the Greater Southwest International Chitlins Cookoff and Jamboree. But I got that flat tire—so I'm here."

When he'd stumbled into the bar, hot and sweaty, Wes had ordered a beer and then called the newspaper looking for a ride. Now he thought better of that—really, there was no place he'd rather be on a Saturday afternoon than a dark, cool bar. He pulled out his cell phone to call the paper and cancel his ride—but the phone was dead. The charge ran out, or something. Wes frowned.

"Chitlins," Jillian said. "Yeah, that's some sort of gut

thing, right? Like menudo, or something?"

Wes thought for a moment. "Menudo is tripe, I think. Beef tripe. Chitlins is chitterlings, or something—it comes from pigs."

"Chitterlings?"

Wes shrugged. "It's all guts, I guess."

"So what are hog maws?"

"They're hog—oh, hell, I don't know. Hog somethings." Wes glanced at the television—men playing golf on cool green grass, lucky men—and then looked back across the bar at Jillian. "Why don't you go on out to Pflugerville for me and find out?"

"I have to work," Jillian said. "It'd be fun, though."

"No," Wes said. He shook his head and looked down at the bar. "No, it wouldn't be fun. If I end up going it's not going to be fun. You know? It'll be deadly out there. It'll be hell. It's 105 degrees outside and I'm going to be up to my armpits in—offal."

Jillian said, "Poor Wes."

"No kidding," Wes said. He looked at the neon beer sign hanging behind Jillian—a rainbow trout leaping for a mayfly—and felt sad. Like weeping, almost. There would be no cool water in Pflugerville—no fame, no fun. Just heat and hog guts, chitterlings or chitlins, menudo or hog maws, or whatever that stuff was, and who wanted to write about any of it? In the 23 years the newspaper had been running his column he had written about barbecue (chicken, sausage, ribs, brisket), country music, tractor pulls, pro wrestling (he had a fondness for old school wrestlers like Ivan Putski and Mad Dog Vachon), ice cream, fraternity hijinks, sorority snootiness, the color orange, rodeo, Juneteenth, Confederate Heroes Day, the NAACP, the Ku Klux Klan, beer (local beer, imported beer, cold beer, the meaning of beer), homosexuals, lesbians, zoophiles, necrophiles, Aggies, airports (airports in general, the old airport, the new airport, funding for the new airport, the land scandal surrounding the place that almost became the new airport, and why the old airport was better), light bulbs: incandescent versus florescent, thunder, lightning, tornadoes, hurricanes, ice storms, floods, droughts, cold, heat, rock'n'roll, nose rings, nipple rings, navel rings (he wrote a penis ring story, too, but the editor said it didn't belong in a decent family newspaper), motorcycles, skateboards, in-line skates, pogo sticks, dogs, cats, parrots, grackles, ostriches, golden-cheeked warblers, fire ants, millipedes, cockroaches, mosquitoes, blind salamanders, tooth spiders, carp, trout, bass, catfish, bats, mice, rats, raccoons, possums, lions, tigers, bears (grizzly bears, black bears, and teddy bears), old cars, new cars, art cars, pickup trucks, and diesel mechanics. He had attended the Budafest, the Wurstfest, the New Highway Fest, the International Barbecue Fest, the Aquafest, the Cedar Chopper Fest, the Sorghumfest, the Pecanfest, the Cotton Pickin' Fest, the Very Best Fest, the Locust Fest, the Big Ol' Bull Fest, the Chiggerfest, and the Crappiefest, along with Catfish Days, Frontier Days, Cicada Days, Buffalo Days, Pioneer Days, Prickly Pear Days, Crazy Daze, the Rattlesnake Roundup, the Chilympiad, the White Bass Run, the Mesquite Burn, the Skunk Wallow, and Spamorama. He had been to dozens of county fairs and stock shows—dozens. Three times a week for 23 years he'd written about colorful, folksy stuff—all kinds of colorful, folksy stuff—and he was popular, and he won awards, and people actually read his column.

But colorful and folksy was getting harder and harder to find: the city had changed, was changing. There were big-assed skyscrapers downtown now, and tech millionaires cruising around in Maserattis, and waves of immigrants from California and Mexico—and everywhere else on the planet, seemingly—had changed the texture of the town. Colorful and folksy, real colorful and folksy, was getting hard to find. Wes tried a few times to write about the new city he was seeing all around him—he wrote about the gentrification of the east side, about inappropriately huge mansions in old neighborhoods, about traffic and traffic and traffic, about air and water pollution, about the loss of friendly old bars and restaurants, and the snootiness of new bars and restaurants—

he wrote columns about the new city, and nobody liked them. They were downers. They sounded like the carpings of a cranky old man. Nobody wanted to read that. People wanted colorful and folksy—at least from him, they wanted colorful and folksy. He went back to recycling old topics. In the end all it got him was a gig as the celebrity judge at the Greater Southwest Chitlins Cookoff and Jamboree.

"We've got the thirteenth-largest city in America," Wes said, "and there's going to be all these people running around worrying about hog guts."

"That's what makes Austin fun," Jillian said. "It's weird."

"That's all a big lie," Wes said. "And I'm a big liar."

"Poor Wes," Jillian said again. "You're just feeling sorry for yourself."

"If you were me, you'd feel sorry for me, too."

"No, I probably wouldn't," Jillian said.

Wes just stared at her.

"Really—I wouldn't."

"You're part of the problem," Wes said. He took a sip of beer and looked at the television. Some rich bastard was putting. He said, "This is going to be the worst day of my life. The very worst day."

★ ★ ★

Three hours later, Wes came out of the bathroom and saw that someone was sitting next to his stool—Heather Kim, a photographer from the newspaper. His ride. He quickly thought about turning around and going back into the toilet to hide, but then Heather saw him.

"Hey there!" Heather said. "Am I late?"

Wes felt gloomy. He'd been getting into the rhythm of the bar: drinking beer, getting teased by Jillian, looking at televised golf, listening to the soft click of balls on the pool table. Saturday afternoon and nothing to do but drink. Saturday afternoon and air conditioning—Saturday afternoon and no chitlins! But now Heather was here and he might have to do something. Work. Eat chitlins. Wes sat back down next to her and said, "I was hoping you were lost."

"I have a good sense of direction," Heather said. She wheeled around on the stool, looking the dim bar over. Heather asked, "Do you hang out here?"

"I don't hang out," Wes said.

Jillian said, "Oh, he comes by every now and then to share his misery."

Wes felt hurt. I have a right to be miserable, he thought—flat tires, chitlins, heat. Now Heather Kim. She was young and relentlessly cheerful, an excellent photographer—an artist, really—who specialized in car wrecks. She was kind of creepy, too, Wes thought, with the wreck thing. The whole area around her desk was plastered with photos of wrecks, torn-up bodies, mangled machines, bloody pavement. Lives lost. Dreams lost. Every time Wes walked by her desk she would shove prints of car wrecks at him. Wes remembered looking at one particularly disturbing twisting metal deathtrap, and saying, "Holy Shit! What were the casualties?"

"Five, I think. A whole family got wiped out—it was terrible." Heather had slowly grinned at the photo, though, grinned until all Wes could see of her face was dimples and teeth. She asked, "Isn't it a great picture?"

At the bar Wes sighed and looked at the television: more putting. He felt—depressed. I have to go to work, he thought.

Heather asked, "You about ready?"

Wes didn't say anything. He bolted the last of his beer and stood up, unsteadily, and looked around. He thought, I don't want to go—anywhere. Not today.

Jillian was sitting across the bar from him on her beer box. She said, "Bring me some chitlins."

Wes said, "You're insane." He followed Heather out of the bar. Outside, the heat hit him like a hammer—the concrete of the sidewalk, the asphalt of the pothole-riddled street, all seemed to bubble and simmer and shimmer under the white heat of the sun. After a moment, even Wes felt like he was shimmering, though he wasn't sure if it was from the heat or from the beer he'd downed. He was sure, though, that it was unpleasant. He put his hand on Heather's shoulder.

"There's a reason bars are air-conditioned," he said.

"Yeah?" Heather looked at him, puzzled. "I guess."

"Chitlins festivals aren't." Wes looked up and down the shimmery street, imagining a world without air conditioning. Desolate, he thought, depopulated—hot and empty and left to nature. No chitlins festivals, either.

"Where're you parked?" Heather asked.

"Parked?" Wes blinked at her. "My car—the tire—"

"Yeah, I know," Heather said. "But I want to see it."

Oh. Heather and her creepy-assed wreck fetish. Wes got into Heather's car and directed her up a hilly side street to where his own car was parked—just where he'd left it, under a wilting live oak, the sad-looking car battered and listing toward the curb on the right front side. Heather rolled down her window and looked at the car.

"Why don't you just change the tire?"

"Can't," Wes said. "I'm driving on the spare—it's the spare that's flat." That stupid fucking donut spare. He'd been driving on it for six months, had already gotten two columns out of the damn thing. Now, maybe, he could get a third.

Wes got out and went over to his car. There was a leaky cooler of malt liquor in the back seat—the moldy back seat—and when he pulled out the 12-pack he saw that Heather was aiming a camera at him. He wobbled backwards.

"Oh, come on," he said. "Don't."

"We need to document the moment!" Heather said. "Smile!"

★ ★ ★

Wes's contact at the chitlins festival was a man named Ben Henderson. They'd talked a few times on the phone, and Henderson had sounded unpleasantly cheerful—as if nothing could upset him. A happy man, a small business owner, a church-goer, something like that. Folksy. When Wes found Henderson standing at the gate of the chitlins festival, he saw that he was right: Henderson was a happy, heavy black man with a baseball cap on his head and a pig-shaped badge on his chest. He stood greeting people cheerfully. Wes thought that something must be wrong.

"Glad to see you," Henderson said. "We were starting to worry."

"Car problems," Wes said. Car problems always explained everything, he'd found. Car problems were even better than stomach flu when dodging appointments or running late—especially when the car problems were real. "So what's the deal with your jamboree again? You're celebrating chitlins?"

"Right," Henderson said. "The committee wants to draw attention to our heritage, you know?"

"Yeah," Wes said. All these festivals looked to the past, to something that might have existed once. He looked past Henderson, to what he could see of the festival—people milling around, puffs of smoke drifting toward him. Wes felt his stomach turn over, rumble; he hadn't had anything to eat all day, except a bag of pretzels with Jillian at the bar. He was surprisingly hungry.

Henderson was talking. "...the proceeds all go to a scholarship fund for—you're not taking notes?"

"What?" Wes asked. "Oh." Wes looked down, saw that he was holding his closed notebook in one hand and a 24-ounce can of malt liquor in the other. He handed the can to Heather and opened his notebook. Then he slapped his shirt pocket looking for a pen. No pen. Must have left it at the bar. He asked Heather, "Got a spare pen?"

"No." Heather dumped the warm beer into a trash can.

Wes looked at Henderson. "Pen?"

"Maybe you can call me back later for a quote or something," Henderson said. "I'll look around and see if I can find you a pen for the judging, though."

"The judging," Wes repeated. His heart sank. "Oh, yeah—I'm a judge."

"Sober like a judge, at least, huh?" Henderson was grinning at him.

Wes suddenly felt like crying—the sun was beating down on his head and depression rose around him and he felt lost and feverish. Fuck this, he thought. I don't want to be here. But he had no place else to go—no way to get anywhere else. Wes could feel his lower lip pulling down, could feel Heather and Henderson staring at him. He didn't want to move.

"C'mon, Wes," Heather said. "Let's go see some guts."

After a moment Wes followed Henderson and Heather through the gate and under the bleachers and out onto the asphalt track that ran around the football field. There were four or five dozen booths set up on the sidelines of the football field, facing the track, each booth with a big pot of chitlins, many people cooking over smoky wood fires, some making barbecue as well, the people in each booth in crazy costumes, music blaring from jam boxes, smoke rising into the pale hot sky. A band had set up under the north goalpost and though Wes could not clearly hear or understand the music he did see a few fools jumping around, dancing in the hot sun. Some sort of Frisbee dog contest was taking place on the football field itself, stupid people hurling plastic disks in the air, dogs jumping and barking and panting. Four or five joggers were doing their laps around the track, going pretty fast up the far side of the field but slowing and fighting their way through the chitlins crowd on the near side. Occasionally the wind would shift and clouds of chitlins smoke blew down the track like a smoke screen; runners and chitlins people in costume would come bursting through the smoke at unexpected times, screaming, attempting to sound like fog horns. There were collisions: Wes saw one runner hurdle a baby carriage and slam into an old man wearing a Texas A&M baseball cap, knocking him down and disappearing around the bend of the track. The old Aggie staggered slowly to his feet and headed in the direction of a booth proclaiming "Department of Public Safety Hog Maws." Then he vanished into the smoke. The baby was left unattended and began to cry. All up and down the row of booths it seemed like people were chanting "Chitlins! Chitlins! Chitlins!"

Once again Wes felt doomed.

Henderson pinned a hog-shaped badge to Wes's shirt that read "CHITLINS JUDGE." Wes didn't say anything; he felt sad. It's come to this, he thought. I am at the end of the line. I too am colorful and folksy. I am a chitlins judge.

"There you go, Wes," Henderson said. "I suppose for right now you can just wander around and look things over. Remember, when you get around to doing the serious judging, you judge on taste, texture, and showmanship."

Wes said, "Showmanship."

"Yeah, the costumes, the booths, the music."

Wes took a deep breath and looked at the mob of chitlins fans. Crazy people, he thought. Folksy crazy. I have to deal with folksy crazy people. In the sun. The afternoon stretched out ahead of him in his imagination: he could tell the day would never end. Wes said, "I'll need drinks."

Henderson laughed and disappeared. Wes looked around. Heather had drifted fifty or so yards down the track, making photographs. A cloud of smoke obscured her. Wes was glad: he wanted to stay as far away from her as possible. She was scary. He started down the row of booths.

The first one was run by a multiracial group of people in pirate costumes. They had a sign over the booth: WALK THE PLANK FOR OUR CHITLINS. They had a Jolly Roger flying over the booth. Wes smiled; he liked pirates, they seemed to have interesting lifestyles. Ride around in a boat all day, sleep till noon, drink free rum.

"Har, shipmates!" he said.

The pirates looked back at him blankly. A little boy pirate waved a sword and screamed wordlessly. Wes didn't feel comfortable.

Henderson appeared with a six-pack of beer. "Here you go, Wes."

Wes quickly slammed one of the beers, then opened another. He left the unfriendly pirates and wandered along the row of booths, dangling the beers from the plastic six-pack rings. Not everyone was in costume, which made things less confusing to look at, though there were enough mad cowboys and soldiers roaming around the field to make a movie—or a war. But now that he was here, and had some beer, he felt he could relax.

But maybe not. Ahead was a booth manned by a bunch of people in clown costumes. He stopped and stared at them. All his life Wes had been afraid of clowns—he loathed them, he feared them, he wished they would all go far away and die miserable deaths. They were awful beings—along with dwarves, nuns, doll-babies, and puppets, they were the scariest things in the world.

"Have some chitlins," a clown called to him.

"Leave me alone," Wes mumbled.

"Hey, Wes," Henderson said quietly, "you gotta start judging the chitlins sometime."

"Clowns frighten me," Wes said. In 23 years he'd never written a single clown column.

He never would.

"C'mon," Henderson said. "Just go on up and taste their chitlins."

Against his better judgment, Wes took a step toward the clowns. A female clown with cat whiskers on her face—and she was a pregnant clown, Wes realized with horror—they're breeding! They're breeding!—aimed a squirt gun at him and fired.

Wes yelled and jumped back, tripping over Henderson and falling to the ground. The asphalt track was hot and dirty and Wes yelled again. He tried scrambling back to his feet—tripping over an untied shoelace and falling twice more—fleeing the clowns, flailing, trying to get away, when he looked up and saw Heather aiming a camera at him. He could hear the whirring of the machine.

Henderson finally steadied Wes and handed him his four remaining beers. "Sorry about that," he said. He looked over at the clowns. "You oughta be ashamed, shootin' the Judge."

"I'm sorry," the biggest, scariest clown said. He was a sad clown with a big drooping yellow mouth and red tears. "Please, come on over and have some chitlins."

"Clowns suck," Wes said. "You guys are disqualified."

A runner came through the crowd and knocked Wes aside and went on up the track. Wes staggered a bit again, but Henderson caught his arm and held him straight.

"Are these kamikazes part of the show?" Wes asked.

"We're sponsoring a marathon as part of the Chitlins Cookoff and Jamboree," Henderson said. "One hundred and four laps around the high school track."

"A marathon," Wes said. He watched a pair of runners dodge through the crowd and vanish into a cloud of smoke.

"I'm not sure who's in the lead," Henderson said. He looked down the track, squinting.

"Why don't you guys just have a marathon like in the old days?" Wes asked. "You know, have some fool run around out in the country for twenty-six miles and then drop dead. It would be a lot more convenient for everybody."

Watching the runners made Wes feel a tad woozy. *I'm* the fool, he thought. Out here in the sun. Out here with the guts. It wasn't the sort of thing he would admit to a co-worker, like Heather, or a Chitlins Coordinator, like Henderson, but there it was: a spot of dizziness hit him every now and then, dizziness, breathlessness, a brief fade and then a return. Actually, Wes thought, the return—the reality—was so awful that the fades were rather pleasant, sort of like taking three or four Xanax with a tumbler of vodka. Still, it was probably unsafe to get dizzy at a chitlins cookoff—there was no telling what could happen. It was the damn heat, and the smoke—maybe, too, all the beer, but that was really just a minor detail. It was the heat that was the killer. He wiped his hand across his forehead and noticed that he had ceased sweating. A bad sign. He thought, I need more beer.

Wes popped open another can. It had been knocked around pretty good when he fell, and when he pulled the tab, beer foam sprayed all over his shirt.

Wes heard Henderson ask Heather, "Is he okay?"

"He's fine," Heather said. She was laughing. "He always works this way—he's a legend."

"How would you know?" Wes asked. Through a gap in the smoke he saw an attractive dark-haired woman at a chitlins booth. He stumbled off in her direction, Henderson and Heather trailing along after him.

Wes wheeled around, knocking over a little blonde girl carrying a plastic bowl of chitlins. Spilled chitlins splashed on Wes's chinos but he didn't notice.

"I wish you people would just leave me alone and let me get on with my chitlins judging," he said.

"You need a photographer," Heather said.

"You need *something*," Henderson said. He squatted down and helped the little girl to her feet. She looked angrily at Wes.

Wes shook his head and began walking rapidly up the track into the smoke. He spotted the dark-haired woman behind a chitlins booth and headed in her direction, dodging two runners and a fat white woman with a tired Frisbee dog on a leash, all the while keeping an eye on the sign above the girl's booth: HENRY'S TIRE SHOP CHITLINS.

"Today's the day!" Wes smiled as best he could and pounded his fist on the booth's table. "I'm in the mood for some tire shop chitlins!"

The woman asked, "Huh?"

"Chitlins," Wes said. He was aware that his speech was a tad impaired, somewhat slurred on the 's' sounds—it was that horrible heat—but felt that the woman ought to be able to understand him well enough. "Chit-lin-sh."

The woman looked around for help. She was darkly tanned and wore neon pink gym shorts. A pink tulip was tattooed on the inside of her forearm and another tattoo—a parrot, it looked like—was half-hidden by her black tank top. The booth was decorated with tires and rims and cans of Fix-a-Flat. A sign said, "Henry's Tire Shop, Hutto, Texas." There was a photo of the tattooed woman sitting on the lap of a bearded fat man—Henry, no doubt.

Wes nodded at a stack of tires. "While I'm here I might as well get my flats fixed, too, please."

She asked, "What?"

"My flats." Wes smiled at the woman. He thought he might be falling in love with her—he had always been attracted to women with tattoos, modest tattoos, and this woman had both a tulip and a parrot etched into her body. She was wonderful. Wes tried to enunciate clearly. "I have flat tires—I need to have them fixed. And some chitlins. Thank you."

The tattooed woman shook her head. "I—I don't know."

Henderson stepped up and put his hand on Wes's shoulder. "He's okay. He just wants some chitlins."

"Exactly," Wes nodded. He had an urge to run his finger across the girl's tulip tattoo but restrained himself. "I'm here to judge the chitlins and to get my *flats* fixed."

"Fix your flats?" the woman asked. But she got out a pink paper plate—embossed with the words HENRY'S TIRE SHOP, HUTTO, TEXAS—and scooped a dipperfull of chitlins onto it. She pushed it across the counter to Wes. "Here."

"Thank you." Wes frowned at the plate of chitlins and looked up at Henderson. "Am I supposed to make notes about this stuff or something?"

"That's the idea."

"I still don't have a pen," Wes said. He looked at the plate of chitlins for a moment. Steaming hog guts in some sort of stewy sauce with bits of celery and green peppers oozing around. He'd eaten worse-looking things—he just hoped they didn't taste rubbery. He took a plastic fork and lifted some to his mouth—and heard Heather's camera whir.

"Stop that!"

"We need to document this moment," Heather said. "You'll thank me later!"

Wes turned away so that they would not be able to see him eat. All his life he'd disliked having people see him eat. He took a step out onto the track, holding the plate and the fork, when something hit him from behind.

★ ★ ★

There was a long period when there was nothing except heat, and the heat was actually rather pleasant. Then he felt someone hauling at his shirt collar and Henderson was looking into his face and saying something.

"I'm fine," Wes tried to say. But Henderson shook his head. Everything was very warm and damp.

Henderson let go of the shirt collar and Wes again flopped over and went face-first into the asphalt track. All Wes wanted to do was go to sleep.

"Roll him over," someone said.

Several hands grabbed at Wes's arms and he felt himself being pulled over onto his back.

"Wow!" somebody said.

Wes opened his eyes—something wet in them—and sat up. "I'm fine," he tried to say. He noticed the tattooed woman was kneeling next to him, holding something to his forehead. The tulip on her forearm touched his cheek. He smiled at her and she grimaced and looked away.

Henderson said, "We got a medic coming."

Wes braced himself on the tattooed woman's shoulder and tried pushing himself to his feet—she collapsed backwards, though, and Wes flailed around and plopped down hard on her belly. The woman gasped.

Wes tried to say, "I'm fine."

The woman said, "Get—"

"Really, I'm fine...."

"Him—*off*!" The woman's eyes were bugging.

"Get him over in the shade," Henderson said. Wes felt hands grab his shoulders and—drag—him over to a nylon lawn chair. He couldn't move—maybe he didn't want to move. He sat limply in the chair and watched the tulip woman get up from the track, specks of black asphalt stuck to the backs of her tanned legs. She disappeared behind the booth, and he noticed that he was bleeding.

Henderson said, "Don't worry, Wes, we got you a medic

coming. You're going to be just fine."

Heather nudged aside Henderson and came in for a close shot of Wes's battered face.

"Go—away," he whispered. He felt somehow congested and was having trouble breathing.

Heather just grinned and leaned forward. She said, "Hey, man, that runner's pissed but I told him we're gonna sue his ass big time for knocking you down. We got the evidence!" She lifted the camera and it whirred and whirred.

Wes kept trying to breathe. Behind Heather loomed the pregnant woman clown, her cat whiskers running a little from the sweat and heat.

"Here's Becky," Henderson said. "She's a nurse."

The pregnant cat-woman clown pushed Heather aside and looked into Wes's face. He shrank back in the chair as far as he could, eyes wide with fear. She peeled away the paper towel that someone was holding to Wes's forehead and a trickle of blood ran into his left eye.

"Can you hear me, Wes?" she asked.

Wes shut his eyes and tried to escape, he tried to fade away, he tried to wipe his mind clean and go home. Still, he could hear: the bass thump of the band at the far end of the football field, the growl of an enraged Frisbee dog, the compressed murmurs and rumbles of the chitlins people. And he could smell: woodsmoke and burning pork, chitterlings, hog maws, chitlins, the soft sweat of the nearby bodies. Wes felt weak, and he sighed.

"Can you hear me?"

Wes couldn't open his eyes. He heard the clown say, "Call 911," and he wondered, why. He wished he was back at the bar, the cool dark bar, watching televised golf with Jillian. He wished he had another beer—maybe two more beers, or three. He wished—something. Something. At the very last Wes heard someone say, "We're losing him."

Riff Raff

At that time I was still making an effort. I was still trying to get my shit together. It was hard, but I was trying. I was driving the cab on a 24-hour shift, hitting the busy parts of the day, hiding in my motel room when it was slower, resting for a few hours before heading back out on the road. When I was awake in my motel room I would sometimes watch television, evangelical preachers in the morning or psychologists in the afternoon, all of them trying to give advice to the poor unfortunates in their audience. All of them spoke at times about *hitting bottom*. They talked about hitting bottom like that was all there was to it—ker-splat, bang, you hit bottom and that's that. The end. Afterwards your life changed, or it didn't. But what apparently none of them understood was that hitting bottom was a complicated goddamn process, that when you hit bottom, you bounce, like a basketball. Of course you hit bottom again, and bounce again, and again, every bounce up a little lower than the bounce before, every smack against the bottom duller and longer than the previous one. It's a process that can go on for a long, long time, and your life doesn't change ever, not usually.

Me, I sometimes bottomed out a little and thudded by a rock house or a bar, but usually I went back to my motel room and stared at the television. I would sit in the gloom and listen to the psychologists and preachers give advice, listen to the people in the next room argue and fuck, listen to the motel owner's Rottweiler bark at whores and children. I was trying. I drove the cab as much as I could.

One Sunday, near noon, my dispatch terminal beeped and I was directed to go pick up someone named Miller, at the Wilderness Road Inn, a seedy motel just up the street from my own seedy motel. I parked the cab outside the room where Miller was supposed to be and honked the horn. Company policy dictated that the drivers were supposed to get out and knock on the door for customers, but I refused to do that. In some parts of town—at the sleazy motels, for instance—it could be dangerous. It is illegal for cab drivers to carry firearms, so instead I carried a long, black, heavy steel flashlight. It was okay for threatening to bash drunks over the head with but of course would not be weapon enough to take on a maniac with a pistol. I waited for a few minutes, then honked again. I put the car into gear and was getting ready to turn around and leave when the door to the room opened and a man came out. Miller, I guessed.

He was pale, almost an albino, pale and dressed in black, with a red baseball cap on his lank white hair and mirrored sunglasses. He had a fax machine under his arm. He came down the stairs and got into the cab.

"You want to buy a fax machine?" he asked.

"No," I said. I started the meter.

"Man, you got a cold fucking no." Miller sat back and laughed. He said, "Listen, pal, I need some extra cash—I need to get rid of this fax machine."

"But you have enough to pay me, right?" I looked at him in the mirror, but I could not see his eyes behind the sunglasses.

"Hey, pal, you think I'm stupid enough to get in a cab without any money? Of course I have enough to pay you."

"It happens." I adjusted my flashlight.

"Hey, pal, not from me. Just stop worrying and start

driving, okay? I need to get rid of this goddamn fax machine. Let's try that pawn shop up the street."

I pulled out into traffic and went three blocks or so to the World of Pawn store. It seemed like the kind of fare that cab drivers hated: driving some fool to a pawn shop for a $3.50 fare, no tip. But Miller was in the World of Pawn only for a moment or two, and he came back out with the fax machine.

"Fuckers wouldn't give me enough for it," he said. "I'm gonna have to take it back to the store—it's on the north side. I still got the receipt. You think that's a good idea?"

I thought: The north side. Twenty or so dollars up, twenty or so back, maybe.

"That's probably your best bet," I said. I started pulling out of the parking lot. "These goddamn pawn shops don't pay anything."

★ ★ ★

The city was quiet that Sunday and traffic was unusually light. I drove north and found the Office Depot Miller wanted. He jumped out of the cab and disappeared into the store. I sat there glumly, hoping that he would be quick. The meter ticked up once, and then again, and again. No Miller. Then an old fat man in a gray jumpsuit came out of the store. He leaned on his cane, looking at me in the cab, then walked over to the Cadillac parked next to me and opened the door. He looked at me again. No one else was in the parking lot—it was as if the streets had emptied and everyone had gone home. No cars, no people, no nothing except the fat old man who was staring at me. I stared back at him. Finally he walked around his car—slowly, slowly—and came over to the cab. I rolled down the window.

"You know, you're parked in a handicap parking space," he said. He had a big bald head and round glasses.

"Yeah?" I asked.

"And you don't have handicap plates, or a sticker."

"No," I said. "I guess I don't."

He planted his cane carefully and leaned over, smiling. He had a huge round head. "Well, you know, I'm kind of an activist for handicap parking rights—my friends call me the Ralph Nader of handicap parking rights." He chuckled and looked at me—proud, I guess, of being the Ralph Nader of handicap parking rights—but I didn't say anything. After a moment, he said, "So, I guess I'll have to ask you to move."

"I'm just waiting for a customer," I said. I looked away at the store. "It'll only be a minute or so."

"Well, then, I'm afraid I'll have to call the police. I'm going to have you arrested." He slowly started to turn away, pivoting on his cane.

"Wha-aaat?" I couldn't believe it. I drive some maniac albino around for an hour, and then I get threatened by an old bald man.

"You're parked in a handicap zone! And you don't have authorization!" The old man took a step back toward me. He wasn't chuckling now—his face was turning red with anger, or madness, and spit flew out of his mouth when he said the word *authorization*. "I worked for years for handicap rights in this city and I'm not going to have my rights taken away by some damn—cab driver!"

"Hey, pal," I said, and stopped. When did I start calling people 'pal?' Miller. Jesus, you drive riff-raff around all day, you become riff-raff—and it doesn't take very long, either. I said, "I'm just waiting for my customer, okay?"

"I don't give a damn about your customer. I'm not going to have my rights taken away by some sleazy cab driver!"

I remembered another driver once telling me that cabs could park in handicap spaces if they were waiting for a customer. So I said, "Ah, fuck you, call the cops."

"What did you say?"

"Call the cops."

The old man's bald head was turning redder and redder. "No," he said, "before that."

"Fuck *you*, I said, *call* the fucking cops." The old man staggered backwards with a shocked look on his face. I hit the window button and the glass rose quickly, and I looked hopefully toward the door, willing Miller to appear. That's how bad my day had turned—I was praying for some goddamn weirdo to get in my cab! As for the old man, let him call the cops. The worst that would happen would be that the cops would write me a ticket that I would stick in the glove box and forget about.

But then there was a *bang* on the rear of the car—and another. I looked around and the old man was beating on my left rear fender with his damn cane. Bang! Bang!

I pulled my big, black flashlight from beneath the seat and got out of the car.

Bang!

I said, "Hey, cut it out!"

Bang!

I said, "Hey, pal, leave my car the fuck alone!"

Bang! The old man didn't even look over at me. He was just glaring at my car, red-faced, grimacing, swinging his cane like an axe. Bang! Bang!

I dropped my right shoulder and took two quick steps forward, swinging the heavy flashlight tight and hard, and I popped the old man right on his collarbone, right at the juncture of his neck and shoulder. *Bang!* His fucking dentures flew out of his mouth and he dropped like a dead piece of meat, cane clattering to the asphalt, his glasses askew, eyes pale in his head. I looked around. The parking lot—the store, the street—was still and quiet, silent, empty, as if under some spell. There was no one around. I looked down at the old man. He was still breathing, I think. The black flashlight was heavy in my hand.

"Hey, pal, what the fuck is this?"

I turned and there was Miller. The red baseball cap was pushed back on his head and he had a big astonished smile on his white face. I could see a blurred reflection of myself in his mirrored sunglasses.

"What the fuck did you just do?"

I said, "He attacked the cab, so I hit him."

"He *attacked* the cab? Oh, man!" Miller laughed. "So let's get the fuck out of here, you dumb shit."

I hesitated.

"C'mon—get in. Let's go!" Miller got in and shut the door.

I tossed the flashlight onto the seat and got into the car. I put it into reverse and backed up, careful not to run over the old man. Miller scooted over to the window and looked out at him.

"Man, you drilled the fucker. He's droolin and shit. He might die or something."

"He won't die." I pulled onto the frontage road and then quickly darted across three lanes and onto the highway.

"You *hope* he won't die. Jesus! I'm in a cab with a killer cab driver. Maybe I should be scared, huh?"

"He was hitting my cab with his damn cane," I said.

"So you killed him." Miller couldn't stop laughing. "Oh, man."

"Like I'm supposed to let him beat on my cab with his cane?"

"Fuck no! Kill the piece of shit!"

"I'm glad you think this is so funny." I kept looking in the mirror, expecting a fleet of cop cars to come chasing me. But there was just the usual light Sunday traffic.

"Killer, hey—get off here at 11th street—I need to check out something over on the east side."

I got off at the next exit and turned left, crossing the highway and heading east.

"I need a woman," Miller said. "Keep your eyes open."

I drove slowly east on 11th and turned left into Crack Alley and went slowly up the block. There were some sullen looking young black men sitting around on the curb watching traffic. Then a drug runner I knew, Wayne, stepped out from behind a car and waved at me. The windows were up but I could hear him yell, "Hey, stop!"

"Friend of yours?" Miller asked.

"I don't know," I said. "Maybe."

"Make a left here and cut over to 12th," Miller said.

"There's no chicks here, just a bunch a crack dealers."

I made a left and went up to 12th and turned right again. We went east past Chicon and then Miller told me to make a left. There was an ancient barber shop with a *No Trespassing* sign in front, and a pair of old black men sitting in chairs. They glared at my cab. Miller rolled down the window.

"Hey! Where's the chicks?"

One of the old men said, "Get the fuck out of here."

Miller rolled up the window. He said, "Dumb pieces of shit."

I made another block and there were three girls sitting on the curb on front of a church.

"Stop!" Miller said. He rolled down the window. "Hey, Michelle, get over here!"

One of the girls—tall, very dark, with short slick hair—got up and walked over to the car. She looked in the window at Miller.

"I remember you," she said.

"Then get in and let's go!"

Michelle turned to her friends. "See you!" she said, and she got in the car.

"How you been?" Miller asked.

"I been okay," Michelle said. "Where're we going?"

"Over to my place," Miller said.

"I want a rock."

"Hey, I don't blame you. Life's stressful. My driver here, Killer, he'll take us to get you a rock."

Michelle looked at me. "I know him—I remember him." She reached up and tugged my ear. "I remember you."

"Oh, man!" Miller laughed. "You know Killer?"

"Yeah, I remember him from some house, somewhere." Michelle got up between the seats, almost resting her head on my shoulder. I could smell the hair butter she used—it smelled like coconuts. She asked, "You remember me?"

"Sure," I said. "Some house somewhere."

"Who was the last back girl you slept with?"

A back girl was cab driver slang—a woman who slept

with cab drivers in return for a free ride.

I said, "Uh, you?"

"Yeah!" Michelle was pleased. She sat back next to Miller. "Right in the back of the cab! Yeah, you're the one!"

"Oh, man," Miller said. "Killer, I'm learning all sorts of things about you!"

"He's a good driver," Michelle said. "He took me out to Manor to see my sister for free."

"Shit, you should've seen him pop this old man a few minutes ago—he drilled the fucker!"

"He beat up a old man?" Michelle frowned. She reached up and tugged on my ear again. "Why'd you beat up an old man?"

"The old man attacked the cab," Miller said. "Killer didn't have a choice. He just drilled the fucker!"

I stopped paying attention. It was like they were talking about someone else—it was just noise. I drove aimlessly—going a block, then a right, a block, then a left, a block, a left, a right down an alley, wherever, whatever. I'd been bad long enough that I knew this part of town fairly well, at least at night. But now, in the daytime, I could see that there were some nice, well-kept homes tucked in along the street, homes probably inhabited by some decent, well-kept people. I also passed three places I knew to be crack houses, full of riff-raff, and a couple more that looked to be full of riff-raff. Finally we came to the house that Michelle wanted, the house I'd seen her in before or something, a big old place with peeling paint and trash bags in the yard. Other trash bags were stapled or taped to the windows and there was a broken plastic tricycle on the front porch. The house was on a hill and you could look west across the highway and see downtown—the capital, the university, the neon-fringed buildings. Civilization. Miller and Michelle went into the house and I sat waiting for them in the cab, the meter ticking up every now and then, ticking up, ticking up. I sat there looking out at the city, the orange sun sinking behind the hills, people driving up and down the highway in ignorance. It all looked so far away.

Mexican Brick

The summer after John Garza graduated from college was a quiet one, at least at first. Years later he would remember how gentle the air seemed in Austin, how the trees in his neighborhood seemed to loom protectively over the houses and muffle sounds of traffic from the streets and from the expressway, how the clouds were so often low and gray and fuzzy. It rained a lot that summer, he would remember. The weather was damp and hot and soft. He remembered the outside so much that summer because he spent so little time at home indoors, for his apartment was haunted.

He first encountered the ghost—encountered, saw, felt, experienced *something*, whatever it was—one night when he jolted awake and saw his dog, a white mutt terrier named Soldier, dancing down the hallway toward the living room. Above the dog was a pale blue light, fist-sized and fuzzy in the darkness, bobbing just above the dog's head, high enough that Soldier's dancing leaps could not quite reach it. Soldier seemed frightened and excited at the same time, circling around backwards with his butt on the carpet, then jumping forward as high as he could and snapping at the air. Garza sat up and watched the blue light move down the hallway into the living room where it rose up toward the ceiling fan and slowly faded. Soldier crouched on the floor looking stupidly at the ceiling—at whatever had been there.

“Hey!” Garza called—not at the dog, but at the light, at the thing.

Soldier raced back to the bedroom and jumped up on the bed and cowered next to Garza. After a few moments Garza got out of bed and went into the living room. Soldier stayed close by Garza’s feet. There was nothing—the usual mess, of course, beer cans and magazines and newspapers and pizza boxes piled everywhere, discarded socks and underwear and junk mail tossed around—but nothing strange. Garza opened the back door and Solider raced out into the night. Garza looked around the dark living room—still, there was nothing. He turned on the ceiling fan to disturb any filaments of the ghost light, and then sat on the couch and smoked a couple of bong hits. Soldier dashed back in and plopped on the couch and leaned heavily into him.

“Whoa,” Garza said, “big guy, big guy. What was that, huh?”

★ ★ ★

Garza’s apartment was in the downstairs of a two-story reddish-brown brick four-plex that was nestled in the joint of a larger, L-shaped complex of efficiency apartments. Separating the two buildings was a dense, hard-packed earth courtyard shaded by three immense live oaks. On rainy days the courtyard would turn to yellowish mud, but there were awnings on the apartment side to keep the walkways dry, and graveled pathways that led across the courtyard to the four-plex and to a little wooden shed that housed the washers and dryers. Weekend evenings Garza and his friends, Carl and Anita Chang, who lived on the second floor of the complex, facing the courtyard, would have barbecues in the courtyard. Garza and Carl and Anita would sometimes be joined by friends of theirs from school, or sometimes a neighbor or two. One neighbor was Rand Kelly, an old drunk who had been a prisoner of war in Korea. He owned the big silvery drum barbecue grill, and so he always hung around even if he wasn't exactly invited.

"That building of yours is made of Mexican brick," Rand said to Garza one night. "I don't know if they brought those bricks up from Mexico or not—they probably made 'em in Elgin or someplace close—but we always call that red-brown brick Mexican brick, you know what I mean?"

"I guess," Garza said.

"It's weak brick," Rand said. "It's sandy. They used to make those bricks by hand, you know? I could probably get out my deer rifle and take one shot and knock your whole goddamn wall down."

"Please don't," Garza said quickly.

But Rand showed no inclination to get out his deer rifle. He sat sipping his Weller, holding a guitar on his lap, staring at the coals in the barbecue grill. The coals still glowed beneath their layers of ash and wisps of grease smoke wafted around. After a while Rand strummed his guitar and sang.

catfish pie
cornmeal turds
in my gumbo

"I don't think those are the words," Carl said.

"Those are *my* words," Rand snapped. "What do you think about that? You don't know everything, do you?"

"I guess not," Carl said. He backed down—they all backed down, always, when Rand said something. Rand was a good thirty years older than any one of them, and drunker, and crazier.

A feral cat they all called Squawker strolled up the walkway, yowling.

"Somebody needs to do something about that cat," Anita said. Squawker was always chasing Anita's gentle little tabby.

"Oh, he don't mean any harm." Rand took a piece of brisket off his plate and tossed it to the cat. "Poor Squawky."

"He's mean," Anita said.

"You think you know everything," Rand said. He looked at Carl. "So what you're in college? I was in college too, before the war—before the *Korean* War." He always specified the Korean War. "Hell," Rand said, "I was going to be an architect before everything happened." Rand nodded at Garza, porch lights from the apartments softly reflecting off his sweaty bald head. "That's why I know about them Mexican bricks."

★ ★ ★

Carl was Chinese, and he was sure that Rand hated him for that.

"So the fucker got starved when he was a prisoner," Carl said later when they were at the bar playing pinball. "So he got beat up. My mom didn't do it, my dad didn't do it—*I* didn't have anything to do with it."

"He's had a tough time," Garza said.

"Fuck him," Carl said. Carl was broad and strong-looking, with wide, powerful shoulders and a big round head. He gunged the machine—slammed it with his hips—and the silver ball hesitated, then rolled over to meet Carl's right flipper. Carl shot it back up through the gate to the top of the machine. "He doesn't like it that I'm married to Anita, either." Anita was an Anglo, tall and slender and blonde. "He's an asshole."

Later, after the bar closed and they came home, Garza waited in the courtyard while Carl went up the rattling metal stairs and around the wooden walkway to his apartment. He went inside and came out with a potato and a broom.

"Come on," Garza said. "Don't do it."

"Fuck Rand," Carl said. "Fuck his car."

Rand owned a beautiful cream-colored 1959 Pontiac Catalina, a massive, flamboyant machine studded with fins and chrome, and Carl had been threatening for weeks to vandalize it—to key the paint, to put sugar in the gas tank, to ram a potato or two up the tailpipe with a broom handle. Garza had laughed at Carl's threats before—they sounded funny, maybe, when they were down at the bar playing pinball or sitting around watching TV and smoking dope, but now, in the middle of the night, with Carl standing there with a potato, grinning drunkenly, there wasn't anything funny about it at all.

Garza went back to his apartment. Part of it was that he was chicken. Sure, he was a coward, he didn't want to get in any trouble, but also he didn't have anything against Rand's car, or against Rand himself. Rand was just old and crazy and drunk—and a racist, too, of course, but what the hell. Soldier was waiting inside by the back door and Garza let him out, then fell back on the couch, staring at the ceiling. He heard Soldier yelp happily, probably at Carl out in the parking lot. Soldier loved Carl. Garza was found of Carl, too, for that matter: they had been best friends for over a year, and did guy things together—drink beer, play pinball, shoot guns, go to football games. Garza had been best man at Carl and Anita's wedding. Except for his weird grudge against old Rand, Carl was friendly and cheerful, a nice guy, a good friend. After a while Soldier came in carrying a big pine cone. He dropped it next to Garza, wanting to play, but Garza lay back on the couch and soon fell asleep.

The next morning Garza was dozing with a hangover and heard a series of popping blasting backfires and then Rand cursing in the courtyard. Soldier stood at the window and barked. Garza got off the couch and stumbled to the bedroom and pulled a pillow over his head and slept.

★ ★ ★

The previous fall and winter the apartment at the top of the stairs had been rented to a girl named Becky, who had gone to high school with Anita. One weekend just before spring break, Becky skipped the courtyard barbecue, and went out to the lake, and she never came back—she was killed in a car wreck. Her death cast a minor pall over the apartments, and over the end of the school year, and over Carl and Anita's April wedding. In June, a couple of months after Becky's parents cleared out the apartment, new people rented the place, an older couple who had lots and lots of booze. It turned out they were married, but not to each other, and had just rented the apartment to have a meeting place for their drunken trysts. One day while Carl was at work—he had a part time job at the library—the couple invited Garza and Anita up to the apartment for drinks, many drinks, and then Garza found himself helping Anita back to the apartment she had with Carl, and then Anita was vomiting, Garza standing behind her with a hand on her shoulder, saying, "It's going to be all right, you're going to be fine."

"Oh, John," Anita gasped. "If only I'd met you before I met Carl."

Then Anita was brushing her teeth and Garza was standing behind her, his arms around her, cupping her breasts, kissing her neck, and then they were on the bed rolling around naked. Garza was drunk, too, but he was still able to think, *Damn.* What the hell am I doing? He didn't stop, though, and for the rest of the summer he lived with somewhat mixed feelings about screwing his best friend's wife four or five times a week.

★ ★ ★

The next time Garza saw the ghost he came awake to find Soldier standing over him on the bed, stock-still, quivering. Garza followed Soldier's gaze across the room and froze. A girl was sitting in the chair—it seemed that way, at least. A blonde girl, a young woman, with freckles, wearing shorts. Garza could see her thighs shining from the streetlights outside the window. She was there, really there, sitting in the chair *looking* at him as if she knew him. Garza's chest felt constricted—he was scared, he began to pant—but before he could move or yell, the girl unfolded and rose up toward the ceiling until she was looking down at him. Then she began to fade. Her blonde hair, her fleshy thighs, her strangely impassive face—all faded away, and Garza was left in the dark with his dog, feeling that something important was happening—something, he didn't know what. Maybe just the possibility of something. Maybe. After a while Soldier plopped down onto Garza's chest, and soon they both fell back asleep.

★ ★ ★

At the next barbeque, Garza asked Rand about the ghost.

"You've lived here a long time," Garza said.

"Twenty-three years," Rand said. "I've been living here twenty-three years."

"And you've never seen anything?" Garza told him about the blue light, about the girl sitting on the chair next to his bed.

"You were having a bad dream," Rand said. He shook his head. "Trust me—I know all about bad dreams."

"I don't know," Garza said. "I think—I think she was trying to tell me something."

Rand snorted. "Your dream was trying to tell you something."

"No, I was awake. I know I was."

"It was a dream," Rand said. "Era un sueño."

"Huh?" Garza asked.

"Era un sueño—it was a dream. That's Spanish. You don't speak Spanish?"

Garza shrugged. "—No."

"Oh, bullshit." Rand was looking at him like he was crazy.

"I took German for my language," Garza said. He shrugged again. Now Carl and Anita were smiling at him. What was the deal? Garza's mother had always been big on assimilation—she wouldn't ever allow Spanish in the house, not even when his grandparents came to visit. Later Garza thought German would be more helpful if he wanted to get into grad school. He said, "Ich spreche Deutsch."

"Yeah, but you're supposed to be speaking Spanish to me. So speak some fucking Spanish to me!"

"Ich spreche Deutsch," Garza said again. "Jesus."

"¡Hablamelo!" Rand was starting to get pissed. He stood up and threw an empty beer can at an oak tree. Squawker the cat took off running. "Hablamelo, dammit!"

"Ich spreche Spanisch nicht," Garza said. "Give me a break."

"Really," Anita said. She winked at Garza and poked Carl on the shoulder. "What're you laughing at? You don't speak Chinese!"

"Yeah," Garza said. He had been sitting with Carl once on the bus from campus, and an Asian student had said something to Carl in a language that might have been Chinese. Carl just sort of shrank back from the Asian and looked confused. "You don't even speak Chinese."

"So?" Carl asked. "My family's been here a hundred fucking years."

"My family's been here, I don't know, *four* hundred years," Garza said.

"Yeah, and they were speakin Spanish the whole time," Rand said. "Fuck all y'all!" He kicked over the ice chest full of beer and stomped back to his apartment and slammed the door.

Garza and Anita and Carl sat quietly at the picnic table. Finally Garza said, "Well, that was dramatic."

Carl said, "That asshole." He got up and began putting cans of beer back into the ice chest. He chunked a piece of ice at Squawker, who once again ran back around the corner of the building. There was still half a brisket sitting cooling on Rand's grill—part of it, at least, was Rand's, for he had kicked in some money for the meat. Carl forked it onto a big piece of aluminum foil and rolled it up. "If he doesn't want it, I'll take it."

"John can come over and have lunch tomorrow," Anita said. She was sitting in the shadows but Garza could tell she winked at him.

In the night Garza woke up, but this time not by a ghost. It was Rand out in the courtyard, screaming.

"Where's my beef? Who the fuck took my beef?" Rand was standing right below Carl and Anita's apartment. "Carl Chang, where is it? Carl Chang, you're a yellow peril motherfuckin Chinaman! You're a beef thief, Carl Chang! A beef thief!"

★ ★ ★

Garza couldn't figure out who the ghost was. He wondered if it might be Becky, Anita's dead friend from high school, but he couldn't think of a reason she would have for haunting him. He hadn't known her very well, anyway. The only real memory he had of her was one evening out in the courtyard when she was sitting with Anita, telling stories about guys they knew in high school, and Carl sat there getting madder and madder every time another old boyfriend was mentioned. He asked Anita about that once, asked why Carl got so mad, and Anita said, "Oh, he always thinks I'm screwing around. He doesn't like to hear about when I really *was* screwing around."

As the summer wore on, Garza began expecting to see the ghost every night. He would sit with Soldier in the dark, in the deep night, and sometimes a light would flash blue, or newspapers on the floor would rustle, or a book would flop over. Only one other time did he see the ghost in human form: it appeared in the door of the hallway leading to his bedroom, a vaporous but clearly female form. It turned and went down the hall, and Garza and Soldier followed, only to see it fade silently into the wall.

Still, the ghost made him happy—just about everything that summer made Garza happy. The ghost and Anita and Soldier—Carl, too, for that matter, and old Rand, and the bars and the beer and the barbeques, and the freedom he had, freedom to do nothing, and everything. It was a big life.

★ ★ ★

A week after Carl ran off with the beef, Anita asked Garza

to come over and help her put up a bookshelf. When he got up to the apartment he found six concrete blocks and a few planks sitting in the middle of the floor.

"I got these blocks over on the side of the building," Anita said. "They were just sitting there."

"I think they're Rand's," Garza said. "He was going to build a fireplace or something."

Anita said, "Oh, come on! Does everything around here belong to Rand? Rand's beef, Rand's barbeque grill, Rand's mean old cat that yells all the time—"

★ ★ ★

Later, Anita asked, "So why'd you want to get a degree in history?"

"I like history," Garza said.

"So? What're you going to do with it?"

"Teach, maybe."

Anita snorted. "History? That's what they give assistant football coaches to teach in high school! That's what they give stupid people to teach—that's why everyone hates history."

Garza lay back quietly and stared at the ceiling. He felt kind of hurt. Annoyed, too. Anita sounded a bit like his mother, who was all the time asking him what he was going to do with his life. When was he going to get a real job? When was he going to go to grad school? Garza had a part time job working at a Shamrock Station down the street. The job, along with what was left of his student loans, was enough to cover rent and food and beer and pot for the rest of the summer, and that was just fine.

"Look at Carl," Anita said. "He's getting his degree in Electrical Engineering. He's going to get a good job. We're going to have a good life."

Garza asked, "And I won't?"

"You should go back and get a degree in engineering."

"Maybe I'll go to grad school."

"*Grad* school." Anita rolled over and put her head on

Garza's chest. "Well, maybe law school would be okay."

They lay silently, listening to the whir of the ceiling fan. Outside faint barking began—Soldier was excited about something. Then they heard Rand out in the courtyard.

"Hey! Who stole my concrete blocks? Who the hell stole my concrete blocks?"

Anita sat up, laughing. "Busted!"

Garza laughed, too. "You know he's going to blame you and Carl for anything that ever happens around here."

"Oh, who cares?"

They dressed quickly. Anita opened the door and peered out into the courtyard. "He's gone," she said. One by one, Garza quickly carried the concrete blocks over to the railing and threw them down. The last of the blocks sort of bounced when it hit the earth and banged into Garza's building, just outside his bedroom. A chunk of the red-brown brick broke off.

"Hey, wow, Rand was right," Garza said. "It *is* soft brick."

"Who cares?" Anita asked again. "Get back in here." She grabbed his arm and tugged him back inside the apartment and shut the door.

★ ★ ★

One day Garza came home from work at noon and let Soldier out, and the white dog raced out into the courtyard. From the kitchen window Garza could see Soldier at the base of the metal stairs eating something out of a dish. Rand usually put out cat food for Squawker. Garza went to the door and yelled, "You leave Squawker's food alone!" Soldier ran back grinning to Garza, then took off again around the side of the building. He came back in a few minutes, and lay down with Garza in front of the air conditioner, and they napped.

Garza woke up from an uncomfortable, bright dream, feeling that something was wrong. His head hurt. He sat up and rubbed at his eyes and then saw Soldier on the floor under the kitchen table. Soldier was lying stiffly next to a puddle of frothy red vomit.

"Big guy?" Garza asked. Soldier looked up at him and started shivering. Garza crossed the room and pushed the table away and sank down on the floor next to Soldier. "What happened?"

Soldier looked at him. Garza gathered Soldier up and put him in the car—he didn't even bother to put on his shoes—but by the time they got to the emergency vet clinic over on Lamar, it was too late. Soldier died just after they got there.

"Poisoned," the vet tech said.

★ ★ ★

Garza couldn't figure out why Rand had put poison in Squawker's food bowl. Rand liked Squawker—he liked Soldier, for that matter. Was he just so goddamned drunk he didn't know what he was doing? He wasn't there when Garza got back to the apartments—probably he was out golfing or drinking. Carl was at work, Anita's car was gone from the lot, too. There wasn't anyone to talk to.

Garza went inside and once he saw Soldier's red sick he broke down crying. Later he cleaned it up and then took a shower and got dressed. It was dark by then. He drank a beer, and then sat out on the back steps to wait for Rand to come home. It was a quiet evening: most of the apartments had been vacant all summer, and were dark and still, and only a little sound from the streets filtered in through the trees.

He heard a car door slam, and then Carl came around the corner. Carl was wobbling a bit; probably he had stopped off at the bar after work.

"Hey," Garza said.

Carl stopped and squinted at him. "John—what's up?" Garza didn't say anything and Carl crossed the courtyard and stood in front of him. "Yeah, I was down playing some pinball—you should've been there, I rolled the machine and got six free games, it was great."

After a moment Garza said, "I've been busy."

"Yeah," Carl said. "Are you okay?"

"Not really," Garza said. Then he looked up at Carl. He didn't want to tell him about Soldier. He said, "Just feeling down, I guess."

"Oh, yeah. Well. Okay." Carl stood uncomfortably, then said, "I guess I'll see you later." Carl walked back across the courtyard. When he got to the stairs, he paused and looked at Squawker's food bowl. "Hey, it's empty."

Garza got up and walked over to him. He asked, "What?"

Carl giggled and lowered his voice. "I put a bunch of rat poison and roach poison and shit in the cat food—four or five poisoned hotdogs, too."

Garza stared at Carl. "That was a lousy thing to do."

Carl shrugged. "Well, that cat—you know?" When Garza didn't say anything Carl laughed again and turned to head up the stairs to his apartment. Garza quickly came up behind Carl and sucker-punched him with his right hand, blasting him right behind the ear. Carl collapsed onto the metal stairs.

"Goddamn dog killer," Garza said.

Carl groaned and tried getting to his feet. Garza hit him three more times—a right, a left, a right—in the face and head, and Carl fell down again and stayed there. Garza began kicking Carl in the ass.

"Killed my dog, motherfucker—*killed my dog*!" Garza kicked Carl until he was winded and then stopped and leaned on the railing, panting. "And I fucked your wife, too, you piece of shit."

Carl didn't move or say anything. Garza suddenly realized—Carl knew. Carl knew the whole time. Garza kicked him some more.

"You piece of shit," he said again.

Garza spat on Carl, then turned and stumbled across the courtyard to his apartment and went in though the back door. He got a butcher knife from the kitchen and went out the front door and around to the parking lot. Carl's car, an older green Taurus, was parked at the edge of the complex. Garza stabbed and ripped at all four tires and when they were flat he dumbly dropped the knife to the asphalt. He went back around to the courtyard and yelled, "Go ahead and call the cops on me, dog killer!"

Carl was still lying at the foot of the stairs, curled up. He raised his head to look at Garza, then ducked and hid behind his arm. Garza spotted the fist-sized chunk of brick that had broken off his building. He picked it up and stepped back so that he had a clear shot at Carl and Anita's apartment on the second floor. He pitched the chunk of brick up, a good throw, and it busted through the apartment window with a crash.

"Dog killer," Garza said. He went back into his apartment through the rear door. He got a can of beer from the refrigerator and looked out the kitchen window at Carl sprawled out on the stairs, then went into the living room—empty and lonely without Soldier hopping around—and smoked some pot and drank the beer. Then he realized that when the cops came to arrest him for beating up Carl they'd arrest him for the pot, too, so he went and hid the bong under the bathroom sink. Then that seemed stupid, because the cops would likely look there anyway—it was no use. He was going to get arrested for something no matter what. He carried the bong back to the living room, noticing that his right hand was bleeding. Then he heard voices out in the courtyard.

From the kitchen window Garza saw Rand, back from golfing and drinking. He was helping Carl to his feet. Garza heard Rand say, "Goddamn, boy, you got your ass kicked! What the hell happened?" Rand put his arm around Carl and they made their way up the stairs and around the walkway to the apartment. Garza got another beer and went to the living room and sat in the dark, waiting for the cops to come.

★ ★ ★

The police never came. The next day the apartment manager put a new window in Carl and Anita's apartment, and later in the week Carl borrowed someone's car and came back with three tires—old retreads, as best Garza could tell.

From the corner of his window Garza watched Carl work. Carl's face was still bruised and swollen.

Garza ran into Anita out in the laundry room one afternoon, but she looked at the ground and brushed by him without saying anything. No one said anything, and Carl and Anita moved out of the complex at the end of the month. No one said anything, except for old Rand, who once drunkenly chuckled, "Hey, you sure kicked that Chinaman's ass. You know that?"

In the fall students came back to town and the complex filled up again. Garza began dating a journalism major named Sherry. He got a kitten and named it Skyhook. He was made manager at the Shamrock station, working full time now, but he came to realize that it really was a stupid job, so he went and took the civil service exam, thinking maybe he could get on with the government. It wasn't until Christmastime that Garza realized that he had not seen the ghost in some months—in fact, he couldn't remember the last time he had seen it, only that he had seen it, that it was real, and that it had tried to tell him something.

Along and Twenty Miles

Then I could hear the distracting mumble of people talking in the hallway outside our motel room. Mumbling, and then someone would laugh, and there would be a pause, and then the mumbling would start again. Every time someone laughed I looked over at Gloria but she was intent on the television, frowning at an old movie, *Samson and Delilah*. I was trying to read a book and the laughing people and their whispered talk were disturbing me. Finally I asked Gloria, "Don't you hear that?"

"Hear what?" Gloria looked over at me. It was easy to tell that she was tired. Seven months pregnant, and a long road trip to a friend's wedding in Minneapolis, and a visit to her parents had all been hard on her.

"Those people out in the hall," I said. "All that talking? It's like they're having a party out there or something."

"It's Saturday night," Gloria said. She looked back at the television. "So they're having a party. You always told me about the motel parties you used to go to when you were in college."

"Yeah," I said, slowly. But maybe not. I looked at the door. It was an awful quiet party, if it was a party. Just that annoying mumble-mumble-mumble and the occasional laugh. No breaking glass, no shouting or screaming, no fire alarms going off, no one racing up and down the halls. If it was a party, it was an awfully boring one.

"Did I ever tell you about the time I ended up in the same motel as an all-woman roller derby team?" I asked.

"I don't want to hear about you having unprotected sex with—circus freaks," Gloria said. "I don't want to hear about any of it."

"I'm just teasing," I said. I put my hand on her big belly and kissed at her neck but she pulled away.

"Bill, leave me alone," she said. "I'm watching the movie."

"I've seen it," I said. "Samson gets pissed off at the end."

"I want to see it," Gloria said. She took the remote from the nightstand and turned up the sound. "These people have just incredibly primitive ideas about women."

"Patriarchal," I said. "Sort of like your dad, huh?"

Gloria glanced at me and then back at the television. After a moment she said, "Don't *you* talk about my father."

I picked up my book and tried reading again. Even though it was interesting—Alvin Josephy's history, *The Civil War in the American West*—I couldn't get into it. Even over the sound of Samson I could hear the murmur and mumble of people in the hallway. I wanted to know what was going on out there.

I got out of bed and crossed the room to the door. I peered out the peephole into the hallway. I could see a black man standing off to my left, sipping something from a styrofoam cup, and I could see an old white woman sitting on the floor across the hall from me, leaning back against the door of Room 122. There were more people down the hall from the old woman; I could see that she was talking to someone. A blond boy of perhaps 10 or so came by and said something to her. The black man said something to someone standing behind him.

I am not by nature a voyeur or a spy, and so I felt kind of weird, watching these people. And yet they were compelling in a strange way. I wanted to know more about them.

I went and took my shorts off the back of the chair and

put them on. Gloria was watching me. I sat on the edge of the bed and pulled on my sneakers.

"Where're you going?" Gloria asked.

"I'm going down to the Coke machine and get a soda," I said. "I want a better look at those people in the hall."

"The people in the hall aren't bothering us," Gloria said. She looked back at the television: Samson was beating up on some people I assumed were Philistines.

"I just want a better look at them," I said. "I want to see what they're doing out there."

"The caffeine in the Coke will keep you up all night."

"I'll save it for tomorrow and drink it then."

I stood up and crossed the room and unlatched the door and stepped outside. Conversation in the hallway stopped. The old lady on the floor looked up at me, squinting, the ceiling lights flashing off her glasses. I looked past her up the hall. There were about 15 or 20 people in the hallway, most of them young and white. They were all looking at me.

"Hey, there," I smiled.

The black guy nodded and took a sip from his cup of coffee.

I stepped around him and went down the hall and passed the vending machines and went on out to the parking lot. It had rained a bit since we came in: dribbles of water beaded on the hoods of cars, and the pavement was damp. The motel was new, built just off the interstate on an old, two-lane farm road, and cornfields rose up at the edge of the parking lot and ran off into the darkness. I could smell the earth, strong and alive, and in the distance I could see the lights of a farmhouse or two, and, on the horizon, a flash of lightning. It was a pretty night.

I walked up the parking lot to our car. I was trying hard not to feel trapped by everything, by life, but I did. I didn't see how else I could feel. A cattle truck was parked across the road at a small gas station. A single steer in the back of the truck lowed over and over.

I said, "Tell me about it."

Our car was fine, locked and safe. I looked at all of Gloria's stuff filling the backseat. I looked at the cattle truck. There wasn't anything to do but go back to the room. The steer mooed again, and I turned and went back to the motel, stopping at the vending machines for sodas. Outside our room the hallway was still full of people talking quietly. They fell silent as I approached.

"Awful tame party for a Saturday night," I said.

"Not a party," the black man said. "There's a tornado watch on. This hallway's supposed to be the safest place in the building."

"Ah," I said, and nodded. I unlocked the door to our room. "I didn't hear about any tornado watch."

"It's been on TV," the old woman said. She had the kind of ugly, grotesque, nasal-y accent. It made my flesh creep. "It's been on TV all night. There's been a tornado watch for this whole part of the state. You don't want to get caught in your room when a tornado hits."

"I guess not," I said. I stepped inside and shut the door.

I heard the old woman say, "Dummy."

I put the Cokes on the desk and crossed the room and took the TV remote from Gloria.

"Hey," she said. Samson was kissing on Delilah.

"I just want to check on something for a minute," I said.

"Give me that," Gloria said.

I searched up through the channels until I came to the weather channel. It showed a radar picture of our area. I could see a big storm—it was colored yellow and red on the radar, with evil-looking purple spots—heading off to the southeast, toward Missouri. I figured it was about 75 miles or so away. Our immediate area was clear, though there were spots of green—light rain—scattered here and there around us, and it looked like another storm might be building to the west. The voice over the radar said something about a tornado watch box twenty miles along and either side of a line extending more or less from Sioux City to Omaha—a line well to our west, and if it kept tracking to the southeast it wouldn't even come close to hitting us.

"There's no tornado out there," I said.

"Huh?"

"Those people in the hallway think a tornado's going to hit the motel."

Gloria frowned at the TV. "Are they right?"

"No way," I said. "Look—the storm's way far away." I thought of the old woman calling me a dummy when she thought I couldn't hear, smug and sensible behind her thick glasses—in that way she reminded me of Gloria's father, a rich man but a smug old maid nonetheless. Sitting in the hallway to wait out a tornado watch. Not even a tornado warning, either, just an ordinary tornado watch. "Call *me* a dummy, that bitch," I said. "Those people are stupid."

"It's not against the law to be stupid," Gloria said.

"Well, it should be."

Gloria shrugged and took the remote from my hand and turned the TV back to Samson. I watched for a moment and then got undressed and got into bed next to her. I picked up my book and tried to start reading again.

"You know," Gloria said, "I'm really, *really*, tired."

I put the book down and looked at her. "I know, honey."

"Don't patronize me!" Gloria turned off the television and looked over at me. "I'm tired of traveling, and I feel like shit. I want to go home, and I want to sleep in my own bed under the ceiling fan in the dark and feel like shit there."

"Hey, I know," I said. I took her hand. I was trying, at least. I didn't know what else to do but try. "Don't worry. We'll be home day after tomorrow."

Gloria pulled away and rolled to her side, facing away from me, and put her hands under her head.

"I want to go back to Texas and lay in the dark, and I want to get this baby over with, and I want to go back to work as soon as I can."

"Okay."

"And I'm tired of all your selfish bullshit, and I'm tired of you just doing nothing but talking all the time, and I expect you to at least try and fucking *help* me."

I took a moment to catch my breath. Finally I said, "Okay, so what else do you want?"

"I want to go to sleep."

"Okay." The light switch was on the wall above us, and I reached up and turned it. The room was suddenly dark but my eyes quickly adjusted to the light from the parking lot as it filtered in under the curtains. I slid my book to the floor and rolled over, throwing my arm around Gloria's belly. I kissed her on the back of the neck and her hand came up and pushed at my face, as if she was swatting away an insect. Out in the hallway people were waiting for a tornado that would not come.

Bluer Even than the Sky Above

Shannon slouched against the door of the car and gazed out the window, focusing on an old black man mowing the yard of a little house set back under the trees. The house looked pleasant and well-shaded, and quiet, and friendly.

"Shannon, you need to sit up straight," her father said.

"I *am* sitting up."

Her father, Jim, glanced over at her, then back at the road. "I hate to see you going around slouched over all the time."

"Yeah?" Shannon looked back out the window at some old people sitting on the porch of an old house, and wished she was sitting with them.

"Really, Shannon." It was Margie in the back seat, leaning forward; Shannon winced when a fresh blast of her heavy perfume overcame the car's air conditioner and wafted around the front of the car. Only Margie would wear perfume on a fishing trip.

"What's the good in sitting up front if you don't use the leg room?" Shannon asked.

"Shannon," her father said.

"Really, honey, no one will respect you if you're slouched over all the time. Boys won't even look at you."

Shannon didn't say anything.

"And when you grow up you'll get a dowager's hump."

Shannon closed her eyes and pretended to be asleep.

"Will you just sit up *straight*?" Her father glared over at her and the car swerved.

"*Okay.*" Shannon scooted her hips back an inch or so, till the small of her back touched the seat. Then she lolled her head against the window. "Sheesh."

"There, that's a little better," Margie said.

Shannon could smell the perfume lessen a bit, and knew that Margie was now sitting back in her own seat—probably sitting straight, too, to set an example. Stupid bitch. Margie made such a big deal out of sitting in the back seat—"No, Shannon, you sit up front with your father, you guys can talk about stuff"—even though Shannon kept saying that she didn't want to go at all—really, who in their right mind wanted to go to a stupid catfish pond?—and even though her father never had much to say to her anymore other than stuff like, "You staying out of trouble at school?" But now her father had said, "We're all going to go, as a family," and he was serious, and for once that was pretty much that. And so Margie sat in the back seat with the twins, perfumed like a department store cosmetic counter—to go to a *catfish* pond—wearing stupid ugly dangly earrings that looked like miniature fishing lures, with a red bandanna around her head and orange mirrored sunglasses across her face, showing off her perfect aerobic-instructor posture. She was embarrassing.

A big gravel truck came down the road the opposite direction, blowing up a cloud of dust.

"What're all those big piles?" Chrissy—one of the twins, Margie's daughters from her first marriage—asked.

Jim looked back at her in the rearview mirror, then ahead at the road.

"That's where they dig up all the gravel, honey," he said. "There's all sorts of pits out here."

"That's where they got the sand for the playground," Margie said.

"That's where we're going fishing," Jim said. "In one of

the old gravel pits."

Shannon smiled grimly and thought about being in the pits, looking out the window at some horses in a pasture. As the car approached them one of the horses tossed his head and trotted alongside the fence. Shannon felt her chest tighten—she wanted to get on that horse and ride off somewhere, anywhere, just *away*, away from Margie, her father, the twins, far away—and she sat up and watched the horse until the car turned a corner and it was out of sight.

"See a boy you like?" Margie asked.

Shannon slouched down again and didn't say anything.

★ ★ ★

The catfish farm was called Bluebonnet Lakes, which were not lakes at all, but merely two old gravel pits out on the rolling blackland prairie east of town that had been lined with concrete and filled with water. They were stocked with catfish once a week, and people came out from the city and fished, and caught fish, and paid for their fish by the pound. Each tank had a fountain that sprayed water into the air, to aerate the water, and there were concrete walkways around each tank, and wooden benches, and a few spindly mimosa trees for shade. In the distance there were huge piles of gravel from active gravel pits, and the south breeze carried the sounds of digging machinery and the occasional dull thud of a blast. The water in the tanks was fetid and dark green.

Jim and Margie led the way down to the tanks, carrying coolers and fishing poles. Chrissy and Cathy each carried their own little spin-cast rod and reel outfits and trotted along behind the grown-ups, chattering to each other. Shannon came last, carrying a can of Diet Dr Pepper and feeling conspicuous.

"Look at all the dead fish," Margie said. "They didn't have all these dead fish last time."

She stopped and looked from one pond to another. In each pond a few dead catfish were bobbing around in the middle. In the nearest pond Shannon watched a black grackle dive down and try to grab a dead catfish. The bird was too small to take the fish, though, and flopped away into the low branches of a mimosa and hissed.

"Well, you know, there's got to be a certain amount of mortality," Jim said.

"It stinks," Cathy said.

"Uh-huh," Shannon said. "It smells like dead fish."

"But where should we sit?" Margie asked. "I mean—"

"I suppose one pond's as good as another," Jim said.

Shannon didn't care which pond they went to, as long as they quit dithering and sat down somewhere. There were a couple of black families fishing at the near pond, and the far pond seemed to have been taken over by a troop of Boy Scouts. She felt like everyone was looking at Margie and the twins and her father and herself—they were all just standing around looking like a bunch of stupid tourists. Shannon took a sip of the Diet Dr Pepper and looked off at the big piles of gravel and rubble sitting on the horizon like a distant mountain range. She wondered what could be seen from up there. She wondered what was on the other side, and wanted to go see.

"Let's sit over here," Margie pointed. "There's, like, a bench and stuff, and a little shade."

Shannon looked at the bench. "You really want to sit there?"

A box of worms had spilled on the bench and the nightcrawlers had dried out and died in their attempt to escape to the shade of a nearby tree. Jim scraped them off into the grass and sat their gear on the bench.

"Okay," Jim said. "Let's catch some fish! Cathy, let me look at your pole."

"I don't know about all these dead fish," Margie said. She had her hands on her hips and was staring out pensively at the pond.

Cathy handed her rod to Jim while Chrissy stood and watched. Shannon felt sorry for poor Chrissy. The twins were not identical, and where Cathy was sleek and compact and bubbly, Chrissy was taller and clumsier, and quiet. Shannon thought that her father and Margie—and Margie's ex-husband, for that matter—fussed over Cathy too much.

Shannon said, "C'mere, Chris, let me see your pole."

Chrissy handed her the rod and said, "The water smells like poop."

Jim had opened the tackle box and spread it on the bench between them, and Shannon was leaning over and looking into it. Without glancing up, she said, "Of course it smells like poop. What'd you think these fish eat?"

"Oh, Shannon," Margie said. "Don't frighten the girls."

Shannon looked up. "Well, it's true."

"No, it's not," her father said sharply. "They feed 'em catfish chow or something."

"Same thing," Shannon whispered. She took a snelled hook from the tackle box and clipped it to the snap swivel at the end of Cathy's line, and clamped on a bright orange and yellow bobber a couple of feet above the swivel. Then she reached for the worm box.

"You're going to put the worm on yourself?" Margie asked. She pursed her lips. "That's so gross. Why don't you have your father do it?"

"Here." Jim reached for the line and hook but Shannon jerked it away from him.

"I'm not afraid of a *worm*," Shannon said. "We dissect pig fetuses in biology class—we have to go inside 'em and find the guts and the glands and organs and all that stuff."

"Oh, Jesus," Margie said. "I can't watch. I'm going up to the concession stand." But still she stood there, watching Shannon and frowning.

Shannon smiled to herself as she ran the hook through the worm, watching Margie from the corner of her eye. When she was done she cast the baited hook and bobber out into the pond and handed the rod to Chrissy.

"Watch the bobber," Shannon said. There was a pair of silver reflective sunglasses in the tackle box and she put them on and slouched back on the bench, arms across her chest.

"Fishing is so boring," Margie said. "Shannon, honey, you need to sit up straight."

Shannon slouched down further and stared out into the green water.

Her father finished rigging Cathy's rod and made a long cast, placing the worm in the bubbly white water next to the fountain. Then he busied himself rigging his own rod.

"We're gonna have us a big ol' fish fry tonight," he said.

"Do worms hurt?" Chrissy asked.

Shannon shook her head. "Not really."

"Of course they do," Margie said.

"No they *don't,*" Shannon sneered. "They're just *worms.*"

Chrissy looked from Shannon to her mother and back again, then out at the pond.

"Yes, they do, Shannon." Margie put her hands on her flat hips and stood over Shannon, and Shannon could smell the perfume even over the rotting fish. "Why do you always have to contradict me?"

After a moment, Shannon said, "I don't contradict you."

"You just did!"

Jim turned around, a worm flexing in his fingers. "Can't you guys just leave it alone for a few hours? Huh?" No one answered. "Shannon, don't contradict Margie, okay?"

"I don't!" Shannon refused to look up.

"Shannon—"

"Hey!" Chrissy yelled. "There's a fish!"

Shannon sat up on the edge of the bench. Out on the water she could see the orange bobber moving against the ripples the wind had kicked up.

"Okay, sweetie, way to go. Now wait till the bobber goes all the way under, okay?"

Jim took a step toward Chrissy and reached for the rod. "Let me have the pole, honey."

Shannon glanced at her father, exasperated. "Dad, let her catch it herself."

"Shannon, don't talk to your father that way."

"Well, he always took my rod away, too. It takes all the fun out of it."

Jim stood back, splotches of red appearing on his face. "Shannon, you were real little then."

"It still takes all the fun out of it." Shannon didn't look up—she was watching Chrissy's bobber.

Margie put a hand across her mouth. "Oh, Jesus, the poor fish doesn't know what he's in for, does he?"

Chrissy took a step backwards and leaned against Shannon's knees. The bobber jerked twice and then went under.

"Now!" Shannon said. She reached around Chrissy and grabbed the rod and they jerked on it at the same time. Shannon could feel the living heaviness of the fish. "You got 'im! Way to go!" She let go of the rod and held onto Chrissy's shoulders.

Chrissy laughed and shrieked and cranked the reel handle. The little rod bucked as the catfish tried to get away, but in a moment or so it was up next to the concrete lip of the pond.

"Dad, get the net," Shannon said.

Her father untangled the net from the ice chest and squatted down next to the water. The fish thrashed and sprayed him with dirty green water, but still he managed to scoop it up.

"Way to go, Chrissy!" Shannon hugged her. "You got the first fish!"

"I got the first one!"

"Honey, don't brag," Margie said.

Shannon got off the bench and squatted next to her father. The fish was about a foot and a half long, pale steely gray and sleek, with black whiskers and a sharply forked tail. Shannon reached behind her and pulled the stringer out of the tackle box and handed it to her father. He unhooked the fish and ran the stringer through its gills.

"Dinner," he said. "We're gonna have us a big ol' fish fry tonight."

"Are we gonna kill it?" Chrissy asked.

"Don't talk like that," Margie said. "The people up at the building will kill it for us." She bent over the fish. "Can I touch it?"

Jim held the fish out to her and she touched it with the tip of her forefinger. The fish wriggled and Margie screamed and jumped back.

"I got one, too!" Cathy yelled.

Jim dropped the stringer into the water and hurried over to Cathy. He took the rod away from her and told her to stand back and quickly cranked the fish in. Shannon watched him and shook her head.

"Get the net," Jim said.

Shannon took the net over to her father. He held the rod high, like the fat guys on the TV fishing shows did, and brought the catfish up to the surface. Shannon ducked beneath him and scooped the fish up as it thrashed on the surface. The fish sprayed her with water, and she laughed.

"You're going to smell like poop, now," Cathy said solemnly.

"Oh, well," Shannon said. At least I don't smell like your mother, she thought.

Jim handed the rod back to Cathy and took the net from Shannon. "This is the biggest one yet," he said.

"Can I see?" Margie asked. Jim held up the fish. "Oh, it's a lot bigger than Chrissy's fish. Way to go, Cathy!"

"I got the biggest fish!" Cathy yelled.

"I haven't even gotten my line in the water," Jim said. He was smiling and happy. "You girls are gonna way out-fish me!"

"Bring it over here," Margie said. "I want to touch it."

Shannon rolled her eyes. "It probably feels like the other one," she said, stepping back.

Jim held out the fish and Margie leaned over and ran her hand along the fish's back. Then she jerked back her hand and jumped away.

"Ouch! It stung me!"

"They've got stingers on their fins," Shannon said.

"Barbs," Jim said. "You have to be careful."

"Nobody told me that!" Margie was crying, bent over holding her wrist. "Oh, *damn*."

Margie sat down on bench and rocked back and forth. Chrissy dropped her rod on the cement and went over to her mother and put her hand on her knee.

Jim glanced at Shannon and stood up. "Oh, I don't think it's too bad."

Margie looked at him. "Oh, yeah, pain's never a problem when it's in someone else's body, is it?"

Jim put his hand on Shannon's shoulder and handed her the car keys. "Go on up to the car and get the first aid kit."

Shannon sighed. "Oh, it'll stop hurting in a little bit."

"What do you know about it?" Margie asked.

The catfish was flopping on the hot concrete and Shannon felt sorry for it.

"Just go," Jim said. He gave Shannon a little shove in the direction of the parking lot.

"I'll help," Chrissy said. She ran to catch up with Shannon.

Shannon looked back over her shoulder. Jim was putting Cathy's catfish on the stringer, and she heard Margie say, "Oh, sure, play with the fish instead of helping me."

"Is she gonna hurt?" Chrissy asked.

"Nah," Shannon said. "She'll be over it by the time we get back."

"Is it like a bee sting?"

"Not even."

They were going around the building and out onto the graveled parking lot.

"How come you know so much?" Chrissy asked.

"'Cause I'm older than you," Shannon said. "I've done more stuff. Dad used to take me fishing all the time when I was your age—golfing, too. And bowling. And we went to football games. We used to go everywhere."

"Wow," Chrissy said.

Shannon unlocked the car and winced as she sat behind

the wheel. The hot vinyl seat burned the back of her thighs and she thought about starting the car to run the air conditioner—and then, shoot, she might as well drive off and leave everyone to their damn catfish. Just drive off. No goodbyes. Shannon was tempted—her father had let her drive once, on a country road out beyond Buda, and she had stayed out of the ditch despite Margie leaping over from the back seat to grab the wheel away from her. She might be able to make it across town—she probably could. But after a moment Shannon shook her head. No. It wouldn't work. They'd just come after her. She sighed. The first aid kit was in the glove compartment, and she leaned over and pulled it out and handed it to Chrissy.

"Here, you carry this." Shannon got out of the car and shut the door and locked it.

Chrissy clutched the first aid kit to her chest.

"Want a snowcone or something?" Shannon asked.

"Sure."

They walked back across the parking lot and over to the concession stand. Some workers from the gravel pits were there, leaning against the banister and drinking sodas, and Shannon could tell they were watching her. She frowned. They got in line behind two boy scouts—the boys were her age, Shannon figured, though they only came up to her nose or so. She looked away.

There was a sound then, a strange animal noise, a bird call, that sounded wild and jungle-like.

"What was that?" Shannon asked.

"Peacock," the woman behind the counter said.

"Peacock," Shannon whispered. She looked around. "Where're the peacocks?"

The woman nodded past Shannon. "Over at that farm over there. I'd like to shoot 'em. Noisy."

Shannon ordered a purple snowcone for Chrissy and a soda for herself, and then turned and looked in the direction the woman had indicated. There was a fence beyond the far pond, and behind the fence were a couple of cows, and some live oaks. No peacocks that she could see.

The woman handed Shannon the snowcone and the Diet Dr Pepper. Shannon gave the woman some money and handed the snowcone to Chrissy.

"Take the first aid kit on down to your mom," Shannon said. "I'll be along in a minute."

"Okay," Chrissy said. She turned and hurried down the sidewalk to the nearest pond.

Shannon watched her for a second, then walked through a gate and stood out on the gravel road that circled the ponds. An empty dump truck bounced down the road past her, kicking up a cloud of dust, and she could hear the men in the truck hooting at her.

Shannon stopped and frowned, and began walking again, scuffing along in the dust.

The road wound around the farthest pond, and Shannon followed it, running her hand along the rough wood of a sky-blue, six-foot fence that separated Bluebonnet Lake from the rest of the world. She stopped a couple of times and peered in through holes in the fence, but she could never see anything more than a boy scout or two, and she moved on. Every now and then she could hear the peacock calling.

The high wooden fence ended and a barbed-wire one began, and there were cattle on the far side of it, grazing under live oaks. Shannon could hear the peacock somewhere off in the distance, under the trees, but she didn't feel like crossing the barbed-wire and getting past the cattle to get to it.

Another gravel truck went by, honking its horn. The sound startled her and she dropped her unopened can of Diet Dr Pepper. It rolled across the road into the ditch. A guy on the passenger side of the truck yelled something but she didn't hear what he said.

Shannon looked around. Behind her, on a hill of rubble, was a sign: NO SWIMMING. Funny, she thought, no swimming on a pile of dirt.

She crossed the road and stepped down into the ditch—waterless at this time of year, and dusty dry—and retrieved her soda. Too shook up to open now, she thought. She looked up at the hill rising above her with its faded NO SWIMMING sign, and began climbing.

The hill was made of big chunks of limestone, and was old—there were different kinds of grasses growing up between the rocks, and mesquite, and prickly pear. About halfway up the hill she turned and sat down beneath a juniper and looked back at Bluebonnet Lake.

At first she just saw the black women and the big crowd of Boy Scouts. She couldn't see her father or Margie. Maybe they've missed me, she thought, maybe they're off looking for me. But then she saw Margie with Chrissy and Cathy, their blonde hair shining in the sun, and she saw her father coming back from the bait shop carrying something in his hand.

She frowned. They didn't even notice I left.

Shannon got back to her feet and went over the top of the hill and down the other side.

There was water in the bottom of the pit—clear deep blue, reflecting the sky but bluer than the sky, surrounded by cattails and willows. It looked clean, so different from the dirty green catfish ponds. A big sycamore was growing at one end of the pond, and there were a number of scrubby trees growing on the interior slopes of the pit—junipers, mostly.

Shannon stumbled down the slope to the edge of the water, ducking under low branches. She sat in the shade of a willow and watched the water. For the first time in a long time there was no one telling her to sit up straight or act ladylike, no one putting her down about schoolwork, no one asking her about boys. No Margie, no Dad, and even though she sort of liked Chrissy and Cathy—felt sorry for them—she was glad to be away from them, too. There were just too many people in her life, too many people trying to mess with her.

She threw a rock into the water and watched the ripples flow to the bank.

"Hey—you a-scarin my fish, there."

Shannon jerked around in the direction of the voice and scooted back towards the base of the tree.

"Don't you be scared."

Shannon squinted at the cattails. Something seemed to be moving back behind them.

"You all alone—right?" A man stepped out of the cattails, a very short man, shorter than Shannon, almost a dwarf, with strange short stubby arms. He had dirty blond hair that was matted and muddy, and a stubble of beard on his chin. His tiny eyes were flat, and pale—they reminded Shannon of the fetal pigs in biology class, of something that was dead and pickled. "Don't you be scared," he said again, and smiled.

No teeth.

Shannon got slowly to her feet and crossed her arms over her chest. She gripped the hot, unopened can of Diet Dr Pepper and watched the little man.

"What do you want?"

"I want you to stop a-scarin my fish," he said. His face was all red and blistered; Shannon couldn't tell if he was sunburned or sick. "They my friends."

The little man had an annoying nasal voice and some sort of speech impediment—he had trouble pronouncing his R's—he said, "fwiends," and "a-scawin."

He threw a little rock— a pebble—at the dirt in front of Shannon, and it skipped past her. She could feel the dust it kicked up on her shins. She took another step back.

"You talk to fish, huh?"

"They good listeners. *You* talk to 'em sometime. Try it—they listen to you. They listen."

Shannon looked at him for a moment before answering.

"I don't think so," she said.

The little man squatted down and looked into the water. "Yeah, they listen to everything I say."

"I gotta go," Shannon said. She turned and ducked under a branch.

"Hey—you can't go!" The little man pitched at rock at her and hit Shannon on the arm.

"Ow!" Shannon rubbed her elbow. He could throw a rock pretty good with his short arms. "Stop that!"

"You can't go!" He jumped up and took two or three steps toward her.

"Leave me alone!"

He glared at her. "I'm not a-botherin you—you just can't go. That's all."

Shannon held her arm and looked at the little man. His pale eyes were wide open and wild. She couldn't tell if they were blue, or green, or what.

"What do you want?"

"What do *I* want? Heck—what'd *you* want? This *my* home. *I* live here. I'm like the troll lives under the bridge. You know anything about trolls?"

Shannon had read *The Hobbit*. "Yeah," she said, "they're stupid."

The little man's toothless mouth dropped open and his little pale eyes opened wide. He looked thunderstruck. He gasped for breath.

"Who told you that?" he demanded after a moment. "Who told you trolls stupid?"

"Everybody knows trolls are stupid." Shannon took another step back, tripping and almost falling over a rock. "And this isn't even a bridge—it's a pit. So leave me alone."

"I ain't a-bothering you." He threw another rock at her feet, and she flinched. "You a-bothering *me*."

The little man—the troll—took another step toward Shannon and she broke and ran, ducking under branches and leaping over bushes and stumps. A small rock hit her on the back and she could hear the little troll yelling—a strange wordless howl—behind her and she kept running, panting, too scared to scream or yell herself, heading around the shore of the little lake, not even thinking to head up and over the hill.

"Come back here!" she heard him yell, and his voice sounded as if he were far away.

Shannon stopped running and bent over, her hands on her knees.

"Come back!"

Shannon saw a stick on the ground, a broken-off length of bamboo, an abandoned fishing pole. She picked it up. It was thin and rattled when she waved it in the air. Too thin, too flimsy. She dropped the stick.

"You come back!"

Shannon could hear him thrashing through the brush toward her.

"Leave me alone!" Shannon yelled.

"I just wanna talk."

Then the troll burst through the brush and into the little opening where Shannon stood bent over.

"Get back!"

"Hey—"

Shannon yelled then and jumped at the troll. She wound up and pitched the unopened can of Diet Dr Pepper at him, smacking him square between the eyes. The can bounced off and tumbled down toward the water and the troll dropped backward with a thud into the weeds.

Shannon looked around, wild-eyed. The troll slowly put a hand to his face and said something. Shannon darted around past him and back through the low brush, heading up the side of the pit at an angle, picking her way across the chunks of limestone and rubble. At the top she rested and caught her breath, turning to look back down into the pit, at the clear blue pond. She heard the troll scream—something.

★ ★ ★

At Bluebonnet Lake they were still fishing. Shannon's father and the girls had their lines in the filthy water, and Margie stood behind them. One of her hands was bandaged. Shannon stood by the concession stand watching them, for a long time. Strangers, she thought. She felt at the left front pocket of her shorts; the car keys were still there, and again for a moment she was tempted to turn and quietly go to the car and drive off—somewhere. Somewhere—not home, but anywhere. But then she realized there was no place, really, to go. Shannon walked back down to the pond and sat on a bench. No one saw her, noticed her: the twins, her father, Margie. It was a lonely world. Shannon closed her eyes and thought about the troll—trolls in *The Hobbit* had been stupid, but they had been *big*, too. The troll at the gravel pit had been—small. She knocked him over with a soda can to the head! Then she wondered if he was hurt, if he was mad, if he might come down off the pile of rubble and come looking for her. What was it like, living in a pit?

A shadow fell across her. Shannon opened her eyes and saw Margie standing framed by the late afternoon sun. Margie asked, "Where've you been?"

"I took a walk."

Margie looked at her. "Awful hot out for a walk."

Shannon said, "Yeah, it's hot."

Margie sat down next to her on the bench. She sighed and said, "I know, honey, you just wanted to get away. This isn't—isn't any fun for you."

"No—"

"It *couldn't* be," Margie said. "It's hot. And it's boring. And you'd rather be with your friends." Margie sighed again. "We'll be going home soon, though. I think even your father's starting to get tired."

Shannon couldn't smell Margie's perfume any more. Maybe it was burned away by the sun, maybe it was overpowered by sweat, or by catfish slime. Shannon shut her eyes and crossed her arms over her chest and slouched back on the bench. She could feel Margie relax, too, a little, and they waited on the bench to go home.

Dry Line

I had only been working at my new job for seven weeks but I was already dreading going to work. Every day I grew increasingly depressed. It wasn't the job itself that depressed me—I corrected billing statements, boring and repetitious and stupid billing statements, for a big law firm—but the woman I worked with, Debbie Peterson, who shared my office cubicle, and who seemed to be slowly, steadily, scarily, going mad.

Each morning's elevator ride up to our office was stressful: sometimes Debbie would show up early to answer the phones until the receptionist arrived, and the doors would slide open and Debbie would be behind the reception desk grinning at the doors, at me, grinning happily but with cold blue glittering eyes. I hated that. I so much preferred to start my day calmly, to step off the elevator into an empty, quiet room.

And on my last day at work, I got what I wanted—got that much, at least. The doors slid open on the fourteenth floor and I stepped out into the little lobby and Debbie was nowhere in sight. A button on the receptionist's phone was blinking. Everything was very quiet.

The west wall of the reception area was glassed in, a giant window, and on clear days it offered a wide and sometimes spectacular view of the city stretching off into the Hill Country. For a week or so, though, the air had been filthy, and a gray-brown layer of smog trapped by the hot early summer air obscured the distant hills. On this day, my last day, I stood in the quiet office looking out, watching the dirty city bustle below me, watching people living complex and enervating lives, watching two yellow cabs blocking the street as they raced to make turns into a hotel, cars backed up behind them on the Congress Avenue Bridge, cars whose impatient drivers were no doubt cursing and leaning on their horns. Farther up the river a bus caught in traffic moved slowly across another bridge, and I could see what were probably grackles and pigeons fluttering in the trees along the river. Directly below me a man carrying a white plastic bag ran to catch a bus but failed. Sometimes you can look out and feel the basic fragility of the world.

"Hey, there."

I turned and saw Ruben the supply manager coming around the corner.

"Good morning," I said. "Look out there, the air's just filthy."

"Yeah," Reuben said. He stood next to me and looked out the window. "Yeah, b-but we do got a dry line coming through later today." Reuben had failed to finish his degree in broadcast journalism at the university eight or ten years before, but he was still hoping to get a job as a television weather guy. "Associated with a low pressure system. Very low humidity on the other side. About mid-afternoon we should see the wind shift around to the southwest, b-blow the smog away, maybe get some thunderstorms." He paused. "I sent out another tape last week, to a low-power VHF station in Nacogdoches."

I looked at him. He was pudgy and short but neatly dressed, with a goatee and a loud red and yellow tie.

"Well," I said, "good luck."

He blinked. "Hey," he said, "I got something for you."

I followed him down a hallway toward the cubbyhole

he worked in. Rueben worked surrounded by boxes of pens, binder clips, legal pads. A treasure room.

"Just got it in," he said. He reached into a box and pulled out a nameplate, my nameplate, *Roy Weston* engraved on some sort of cheap gold-tinted metal. "Now you're officially an employee of Cox O'Brien."

"That's good, I guess," I said. I was pleased, though. The nameplate felt good in my hand. This was the first real job I had had in almost four years, since I'd gone broke and sick and hit bottom the first time, and even though I was just a billing clerk—a ridiculous billing clerk, for Christ's sake—I not only liked this job, I wanted it, and needed it.

"Debbie's looking for you," Reuben said.

"Oh." My heart sank. I looked at Rueben but he was already busy at his cluttered desk. "Did she say what she wanted?"

"Nah," Reuben said. "Not really—she said she had something to show you. I don't know what. Something."

Oh well. I looked around Reuben's shelves for a moment and grabbed a new Cox O'Brien mouse pad and a box of binder clips and then headed on to work.

Did Reuben ever notice anything about Debbie? Anything odd? I guessed not. None of the other people working there ever seemed to talk about her. Debbie was always bright and cheerful and apparently well-liked, and I wondered if maybe she confided her delusions to me alone.

★ ★ ★

Cox O'Brien was the largest law firm in Austin, and one of the two or three largest in the state, and took up four floors of the building. My boss bragged to me once that some of the attorneys were famous, and some were retired legislators, and many were millionaires, as if all that would impress me, but I'm pretty sure I never saw an attorney while I was working there. As far as I could tell we lived in different worlds. My life at Cox O'Brien was lived in a long series of rooms running along the east side of the fourteenth floor. There was a big room walled into cubicles where Debbie and I worked with five other people in Accounts Receivable, a narrow hallway leading past Terrence's office and the big boss's office, the break room, and a pair of accountants' offices, and then another big open room for the Accounts Payable squad. From our windows we could look away to the highway and the convention center and the poor neighborhoods of the east side.

Debbie was sitting at her desk talking on the phone when I came around the corner of our cubicle. *I'm looking for you,* she mouthed and pointed at me. I nodded and slid into my chair. I stared out the window.

Debbie had come back from maternity leave just a couple of weeks before I was hired, and when I got there I had endured seemingly endless talk about her new daughter, and though she never mentioned the baby's father I assumed there was one somewhere. Then after about a week Debbie asked me what I thought about reincarnation. I told her I tried to keep an open mind about such things. Then she started to tell me about her past lives. She remembered a lot of them. The only one that impressed me was a 19th century incarnation where she was Friedrich Nietzsche's mother. She said he had been a cheerful and uncomplaining child.

Debbie hung up the phone. "Good morning," she said to me.

I glanced at her. The firm was big on appearances, and had a dress code, but somehow the dress code never applied to Debbie. Her clothes were never very clean but today they were dirtier than usual: a pair of too-tight yellow stretch pants had a big smudge of something oily on the left thigh, and her lime green top was also smudged and fraying around the sleeves. It was like she'd never picked up any hygiene habits in any of her past lives. I wheeled my chair around and looked back out the window. A fire was burning over on the east side—a thin column of black smoke was rising through the brown haze and drifting with the southeast breeze.

"The air's filthy today," I said.

Debbie looked up and out the window. "Yeah? I guess so."

"Reuben says a dry line might come through this afternoon, though."

"Reuben's strange," Debbie said. She wheeled her chair over next to me. She was wearing perfume but beneath that she smelled like old teabags. "Look at this."

She carefully placed a ¾ inch machine screw on my desk. I looked from the screw to Debbie's face. Her pale left eyebrow was arched.

I said, "It's a screw."

"I found that in the street outside my house," Debbie said. "Gypsies. They're trying to give me flat tires."

"Ah," I said. "Yeah, the gypsies."

The gypsies. Debbie had three topics of conversation: her daughter, reincarnation, and the gypsies. Debbie—or Debbie's spirit or soul or whatever—had done something to annoy the gypsies centuries ago, and they had been pursuing her through different times and incarnations ever since. I never knew what to say about the gypsies. She told me she carried a pistol at home to defend herself against the gypsies—she said she was ready to kill them—but I just hoped she wouldn't bring it to work and get confused and shoot me or our co-workers.

I picked up the screw and handed it back to her. I said, "Yeah, that could cause some damage, all right."

"I know." Debbie pushed her chair back across the cubicle. "It's just—they never stop, never. The gypsies are just trying to—to get me." She put the screw in her paperclip holder and stood up. "I tried telling my mother about this—I tried. She said—do you believe this?—she said I should see a doctor! I don't need a doctor—I need a bodyguard!" Debbie headed for the break room, farting as she rounded the corner of the cubicle.

I got up and slid my nameplate into the slot at the top of our cubicle's wall. When I looked across the room I saw my boss, Terrence Bailey, a tall, heavy, pear-shaped black man, enter the work area and head toward his office. I waved at him but he didn't seem to see me, or he didn't want to see me. I sat back down and glanced out the window once more before settling into the pile of work on my desk.

★ ★ ★

Later Debbie said, "Donna keeps sticking her fist in her mouth. You have any idea why?" Donna was her new daughter.

"Really," I said, "I don't know anything about babies."

"I feed her, you know? She shouldn't be hungry."

I shrugged and tried to get some work done. I tried to concentrate. As creepy as the gypsies were, they were more interesting than Debbie's daughter.

"And she's too young to be eating meat, anyway. She doesn't even have teeth."

I finally looked up. "You think she's trying to eat her own fist?"

"That's just it!" Debbie said. "I don't know what she's doing! She keeps sticking her fist in her mouth and I don't know why!"

Debbie got up and paced to the edge of the cubicle and back. She sat heavily in her chair and placed her head in her hands and began to cry.

Terrence the boss lumbered over—blubbery, knock-kneed, his wide hips swaying.

"Everything going okay?" he asked Debbie.

"Donna wants to eat *meat*!" Debbie said. She grabbed a tissue and dabbed at her tears.

Terrence chuckled. "Kids sure grow up fast," he said. "She must be getting big." He wouldn't look at me.

"I think we'll get the rest of these bills out today," I said to him. Cox O'Brien was defending a tire company that manufactured defective tires. Twenty or so people had been killed, scores more injured, and there were hundreds of lawsuits. Everybody at the firm was very happy.

"Just keep at it." Terrence said to Debbie. He walked slowly back to his office.

Debbie sniffled a few times and started in on the gypsies again. I tried to shut her out and do my work. I was supposed to correct the grammar, spelling, and punctuation on the different billing statements before we printed them and mailed them out. The ancient billing software we used had editing functions that were clunky and complicated, but, really, the work was pretty easy as long as I paid attention. As long as I concentrated. A couple of weeks earlier Debbie had been telling me how she was falling down a lot—the gypsies were coming into her house at night and moving the furniture around, and she would trip and fall—and how the gypsies had stolen some of her underwear, and how her daughter, Donna, had been her sister back in the 16th century, and how little Nietzsche had just said the cutest things as a child—and in the middle of all this I let myself get distracted and I printed off some statements with incorrect addresses and misspelled plaintiff names. The lawyer handling the cases had apparently been very *very* pissed, and he fussed at the big boss, who fussed at Terrence, who called me into his office and fussed at me. There was nothing I could say, though. It wasn't Debbie's fault. She could rattle away about all sorts of crazy weird shit and still put out twice as many billing statements as I could, and they were always perfect.

★ ★ ★

I sat my desk in the late afternoon working on those tire company statements when my phone rang. It was Terrence. He asked me to meet him down in the personnel office on the 13th floor. Debbie was in one of her silent moods, staring at her computer screen, entering data with one hand, thoughtfully fingering the gypsy screw with the other.

"I have to go down to personnel for a minute," I said. She nodded.

I went out to the reception area and down the spiral

staircase that led to the 13th floor. Through the glass wall I could see storm clouds building out to the west—the dry line Reuben had promised.

The personnel manager was a tiny, thin, frowning woman named Toni. She told me to shut the door and take a seat, and when I did, Terrence glanced at her and then looked at the floor and said, "Roy, I don't know how to tell you this—I hate this—but we have to let you go."

I sagged. For a moment I felt like I had been shot. But, still, strangely, I wasn't surprised. I'd lost just about everything over the years through my own carelessness and idiocy and depression, and everything I hadn't lost had been taken away from me. Even with the fancy new nameplate, I couldn't be surprised that something bad was happening.

I said, "But you told me last week I was doing fine."

"That was last week," Terrence said.

"What changed?"

"Nothing—"

"Then what happened?"

Toni said, "We just want what's best for the firm."

"We want the best *fit*," Terrence said quickly.

I just looked at him. The fat sack of shit. "Last week you said I was a fine fit."

"I was speaking personality-wise," Terrence said.

Again Toni said, "We just want what's best for the firm."

"Personality-wise you're a fine fit."

I said, "I haven't made a single error since I screwed up those statements a couple of weeks ago, and you know it."

"The firm wants the best fit," Toni said.

"Personality wise, you're fine," Terrence said. "But work-wise—"

Toni said, "Terrence tells us you're sort of slow—"

"I'm still learning the programs," I said. "I'm concentrating on accuracy."

"—and that you don't take notes during meetings."

"Notes." I looked at Toni, astonished, and then at Terrence. Yes, Terrence had told me a couple of times to take notes in the meetings. But why? All that ever happened in meetings is that Terrence's boss, the big boss, would chortle about defective tire suits or air pollution suits or some other calamity for mankind that was bringing the firm more business and more money. "That's all? *Notes*?"

"You're still in your 90-day probationary period, Roy," Toni said. "We can terminate you if we don't like the way you smile, if we want to."

"Notes?" I still couldn't believe it.

"Debbie takes notes," Toni said. "And she's faster and more accurate than you are."

Terrence said, "What we were looking for, really, is another Debbie."

"Debbie—" I began. Is fucking insane. But I didn't say it.

★ ★ ★

After I signed the papers Toni pushed at me, I followed Terrence back up to the work area. We took the elevator, and were alone. I looked at him.

"You really are a big fat lying sack," I said. "Fucking notes!"

He pursed his lips for a moment, then said, "Please don't get personal, Roy."

"You lied to me—you told me last week I was doing great."

"That was last week." Terrence looked at the floor.

"What changed?"

"Nothing." He wouldn't look at me.

"Liar."

The elevator opened and Terrence wobbled off to his office and closed the door. I went over to my cubicle. The nameplate was shining on the wall in its little holder and for a moment I felt like hunting Terrence down and smacking him with it. But then a wave of sadness came over me, a wave of futility and depression. I slid the nameplate out and tossed it down on my desk.

"I have to go," I said to Debbie.

She looked up from her desk. I must have looked pretty bad, because she immediately guessed what was wrong. "No—they fired you. They didn't!" She got to her feet awkwardly. "The bastards."

I started to cry. I didn't say anything.

"That bitch Toni in personnel is a gypsy," Debbie said quietly.

I took one of Debbie's tissues and dried my own tears. I said, "I think she's Mexican."

"*Gypsy.*"

I shook my head and began gathering up my things—a couple of photos, some notebooks, that damn nameplate—and sticking it all in my knapsack. I thought for a second and then stuck the new mouse pad and the unopened box of binder clips in as well.

"She better not come after me," Debbie said. "I'd kill her if she came after me. I have a daughter to support."

I didn't care. I zipped up the knapsack and turned and stuck my hand out to shake with her. I said, "Well."

Debbie shoved my hand aside and hugged me tight. "You're a very old soul, Roy," she said. "I've known you in many lives. Don't worry. This was meant to be."

I was pretty sure it wasn't, but I didn't feel like arguing. I looked across the work room and saw Terrence standing in his office doorway, watching me. When he saw me see him, though, he quickly stepped back and shut the door. Fat lying sack. I pulled away from Debbie, from the smell of her perfume and dirty clothes—away from the gypsies and Nietzsche and the meat-eating baby.

"I'll be in touch," I said.

"Listen," Debbie said. "When you apply for a new job, don't leave Terrence for a reference—leave me. I'll say you were great. I'll say I've known you for years!"

"Thanks," I said.

I walked out to the reception area. The pretty girl behind the desk smiled at me. "Going home early?" she asked.

"My lucky day," I said.

Once I got on the elevator I began crying again, weeping until the fifth floor when two older men in expensive suits got on. I rubbed at my eyes and mumbled something about allergies, as if they cared.

Outside it was noisy and humid and I found it hard to breathe. Despite the activity and noise of the street I felt as if a tomb was closing over me. The wind was picking up, a little, shifting around to blow from the southwest, and the sky was dark. My eyes were watering again, and I wondered if it might really be allergies, or the air pollution. I crossed the street toward the bus stop and a light pattering of rain began, steaming on the hot pavement, but it stopped, stopped before I got to the other side.

Wildlife Rehabilitation

Where I live in Texas the hills level out and rise into the plains and the sky opens up to swallow everything. In the fall and winter fronts blow through, cold dark clouds and wind rattling the brush and pushing birds down from the north—most notably, great numbers of hawks and eagles. When I was a young man, people hated those birds. In those days, between World War II and Korea, it was not an uncommon thing to see dead eagles and hawks strung up on fence posts along our roads, shot dead and left to rot, a warning to all other varmints. Crows and buzzards would drift by and pick at the carcasses, and most of the dead birds' feathers would float off into the brush, and finally, after a few months, by summertime, all you'd have left to see would be maybe a skeleton with one wing and a head, hanging there from a clawed foot like a grim vision of the future that awaits us all. It was something to see, all the dead birds hanging from fence posts, but it's not so common anymore. In fact, it's not something I had seen in years, or even thought of, until my cat—his name was Festus—was killed by my neighbor's golden eagle.

Instead of keeping dogs or cats, like normal people, Vernon and Merrill Brown kept birds—hawks, owls, buzzards, eagles—they even had a caracalla, which people around here call a Mexican eagle. Vernon called himself a "Wildlife Rehabilitation Specialist," though what he did for a living was clean out the kennels and stables for our local vet. People who found injured birds would bring them in and Vernon would try to fix them up so that they could be released. He even had a federal permit to keep them. The birds lived in big wire pens in his garage, but Vernon brought them outside most days, tethering them to the clothesline poles in his backyard. My backyard faced his, our properties separated only by an eighteen-inch garden-wire fence, and I could stand in my kitchen and watch the birds. They would flap their wings and preen, showing off, like they thought they were so big and important.

One day, when we were still speaking—that is, before my cat was killed—Brown added a great horned owl to his little aviary. It had been shot and wounded to the point where he and Dr. Jordan decided it might never be able to hunt again, and he kept it in its own special corner of his garage. Of all the birds Brown kept, I liked that owl the best. I liked its big yellow eyes and how it bobbed its head around when it watched me, and I told Brown how the Comanches—our town is named for them—had a lot of myths and stories about owls, how they thought owls were inhabited by bad spirits, how they told stories about the terrible Cannibal Owl. Brown thought all that was pretty good, and he showed me how he fed the owl. He used dead mice.

"Not hamburger or just old raw meat?" I asked.

"Not enough vitamins," he said. "They need the guts and the bone marrow and all that good stuff."

I asked him why he didn't use live mice and let the poor old owl have some fun hunting down his food, and Brown said that it wouldn't be any good to have an owl flapping around the garage killing things, and besides, my Festus was keeping the mouse population down.

Brown bought the mice alive out at the pet department at the Wal-Mart, and then he'd bring them home and put them in a box and lower them into his deep freeze and kill them. He showed me the whole thing—the box of white mice, the deep freeze. When he opened the freezer to show me, he had two dead screech owls in there he was planning to do some taxidermy on when he got around to it, a brisket he'd bought when they had that sale at Lone Star Meats, a box of fish sticks, a big bag of frozen peas, and four or five frozen pizzas. And he had this cardboard box full of white mice, a dozen or so of them, you could hear their little feet scratching around on the inside of it, and he sat the noisy box down in the deep freeze on top of a deluxe meat and cheese pizza, and he closed the lid.

We went inside then for dinner—like I said, we were on speaking terms, then, friends, even—and Merrill had made a pot roast, with mashed potatoes, and gravy, and peas, and biscuits, and it was all pretty good, too. But all the time I was eating I was thinking about those damn mice freezing in that dark, cold box.

Merrill, meanwhile, was talking about working with birds. "Now, herons are dangerous," she said. Merrill was a big woman—not fat, but tall and broad-shouldered and bosomy, with a long nose and thick black hair. "Very dangerous."

"Herons?" I asked. I'd seen a few herons around the Leon River and Proctor Lake and over on Lake Brownwood. They never looked too vicious to me.

"Herons," Brown said. "Green herons, great blues, night herons." Brown had a long, stringy beard that reached halfway down his chest. Every time I looked at him I was afraid I would see chunks of mashed potatoes lodged in his beard, or maybe insects crawling around in it, or bird shit, or whatever. Merrill was much easier to look at.

"You always have to wear goggles when you work with herons," Merrill said. "They'll peck at anything that moves, like your eyeballs."

"Well," I said. "I guess we live in an unfriendly world." I thought again of the mice in the freezer—of the owl that would like to pounce on them if it could. The dead hawks hanging on fence posts—hell, I thought then of all the people I'd known hurt or maimed by animals, stepped on by cows, kicked by horses, bit by dogs. People struck by lightning, people drowned in flash floods. People smashed in car wrecks, men I'd seen blown up in Korea. My wife dead of cancer, too. There were bodies everywhere, really, if you looked hard enough and thought about it. Herons and eyeballs, I thought. Jesus.

Merrill and Vernon were staring at me. I guess I'd been silent a long time, paused, holding my fork in mid-air.

"Well," I said to them, "I'm glad we didn't have any damn herons around here when I was working at the pharmacy." They all laughed, but my mind was still out there in the deep freeze, and with every other dead creature I'd known. "I guess we did have some old ladies who'd come in and peck around, though," I added, and they laughed harder.

I think of that evening now, of those frozen mice, of Merrill and Vernon laughing, and of me feeling welcome and appreciated, and I just feel sick inside.

★ ★ ★

During the time my wife, Margaret, was ill, was dying, Festus was my best friend, my comfort. He was gray with darker gray and black stripes, short haired. Margaret found him just after she found out she had cancer, found him shivering in the drizzle under some bushes outside the clinic in Fort Worth where they'd done the biopsy. I told her I didn't need a damn cat around the house, what with her sick, but she stuck the cat in her purse anyway and we drove home in the rain and the kitten crawled out of the purse and across the seat and nestled in my lap, right in my crotch. Sick as she was, Margaret thought that was pretty funny. I said I supposed we could keep the damn cat as long as he didn't try nursing on me or anything.

We named the cat Festus after the guy who rode the mule on "Gunsmoke," which we still watched on reruns on the cable TV, and he grew up to be a handsome cat, slender and agile, and though he had the run of the neighborhood, and his own little door I fixed in the front window, he always came home at night and slept with us, laying straight between Margaret and me, heavy and warm and alive and loving.

Margaret lived another three years before the cancer finally spread to her lungs and killed her. And she had a pretty good life, right up till the last few months, when, as most anybody who has lost someone to cancer knows, things turned gruesome. I spent my whole working life as a pharmacist and I thought I might somehow be of help, might know something, but I was nothing but helpless, and stupid—and depressed, I guess, and many nights I would sit in the dark with Festus purring close and warm, Margaret in the hospital dying, and I felt bad. He was a good cat. He was a comfort. He was my friend—something that Vernon and Merrill Brown would never understand. Festus was a friend, not a toy or a *thing*. My friend.

★ ★ ★

For a long time just after Margaret died everyone was very kind to me. People brought me all sorts of things to eat—my God, they brought casseroles, and fried chicken, and roasts, and pies, and who knows what all, though of course I never did eat much of anything, my appetite dropped to almost nothing, and I got skinny. But all sorts of people came by the house after Margaret's death. She was a very popular woman. She'd taught school for thirty years, fourth grade, mostly, and was always busy with church and with the garden club, and she was a poll-watcher for the Democratic Party until she switched over to the Republicans and became a poll-watcher for them. And so the Republicans came by the house, a dour bunch, and the church people, and her garden club friends—Margaret's friend Donna Bradshaw kept offering to come over and prune the roses for me, as if I was incapable of pruning a damn rose. Ex-students came—after all those years, half the town was ex-students—and lots of neighbors. My friend James brought me a bottle of Weller's and we sat and drank whiskey in the front room while people milled around the kitchen. Festus came and hopped on my lap and I petted him and held him tight. My son, Brian, the big shot insurance salesman, was on the phone half the time "making arrangements" —arrangements for what I don't know, since Margaret had planned and arranged her own funeral when she learned of her cancer—while the grandkids were out in the back yard staring across the little fence at Brown's birds—the two hawks, the big owl, and the caracalla. James made some comment about circling buzzards that I only half-caught but that Donna Bradshaw thought was terrible, so terrible that she had to leave, which caused me to thank James. Then I saw Brown and Merrill in the kitchen talking to some people, and Merrill came in and sat next to me and took my hand away from purring Festus and squeezed it, and held it in her lap.

"If you ever want anything, just call me," she said.

James heard that and winked at me. I ignored him and looked at my hand in Merrill's lap.

"I appreciate that," I said. "You and Vernon have been good neighbors to me."

And so I ended up having dinner over at their place a couple of times a week that fall and winter, listening to them talk about birds while I avoided looking at Brown's beard and thought about all those poor mice dying in the deep freeze.

★ ★ ★

It was the next spring when Brown got the eagle. I looked out the window one afternoon and saw him with it there in his back yard, and I had to go out for a better look. Outside of those dead and dried ones hung from fence posts in the past, I had never seen an eagle up close. I went out the back door and across the yard and I stepped over the short fence and walked up to Brown. He was looking up at the eagle, admiring it.

"That's an eagle," I said. "It's a golden eagle, right?" People sometimes called them black eagles.

"Yep," Brown said. He adjusted the tether around the bird's ankle—the tether that soon proved to be too goddamned long—and he turned and looked at me and smiled. Brown's beard fluttered in the wind and I felt uneasy looking at it, so I looked at the bird.

"My God," I said. It really was an impressive and beautiful animal. It had eyes that were feral and strange, wild like a mad dog but cold. The spring wind ruffled feathers on its cape and it opened its wings and they were just huge. And its feet—its claws, its talons—were big, too. As a child I always heard stories about eagles carrying away sheep or calves—or sometimes even attacking children. People hated eagles then, killed them every chance they got—from airplanes, even—and I think now they were probably right to do so. "My God."

"Some asshole shot it," Brown said. "Deputy found it and turned it over to Dr. Jordan." Ted Jordan was the vet that Brown worked for. I used to take Festus to him. "We pulled out a handful of number six shot, but he'll be okay."

The eagle flapped then and silently opened his mouth. His little pink tongue looked like a worm. I took a step back.

"Number six?" That's what I used to use for dove hunting. "I wouldn't think that'd bring down an eagle."

"Shot 'im up close," Brown said. "They're not always afraid of cars. You just drive up and wham!"

The eagle flapped his wings again, and I could see where he had been shot—his left shoulder was missing some feathers and that wing did not seem as powerful as the other.

"My God," I said. "Just think."

★ ★ ★

Within a few weeks I got used to seeing the eagle in Brown's back yard. It sat on its pole like it actually belonged there. But then late one afternoon—early evening, I guess, for it was getting dark—I looked out and the eagle was not on his perch but on the ground, with his wings spread wide.

I thought that was odd. I went out the back door and down the steps and began crossing the yard, and I could see the damn eagle tearing at something—I saw some grayish fur, then, and I began running as much as I could run, slow, crossing the grass, staggering over the little fence that separated our yards, and there was that damn eagle sitting atop my cat, my Festus. One huge claw was around my cat's head, the other back in the grass for balance, and the eagle was tearing at his guts. The eagle looked up at me with some intestine dangling from his mouth and I kicked him square in the chest.

"Get out of here, you piece a shit!" I yelled.

The eagle flopped back from my kick and screeched and flopped his great wings some more. I guess he would have tried to fly but he had that hurt shoulder from being shot and that tether around his foot and so all he did was flop and thrash. I kicked him once more and then I heard Vernon shout something from the window. I ignored him, though, and bent over my cat. He was dead, dead with his poor guts ripped out and half-eaten.

"Aw, kitty," I said.

I picked him up and he was warm and limp, and there was cat blood everywhere, and the warm smell of guts. The damn eagle was still flopping around, trying to catch his damn balance or something, and then Vernon was outside, and he said, "What happened?"

"Your damn eagle killed my cat," I said.

"No." His mouth gaped open and his beard waggled in the wind. Sickening. Sick.

I glared at the son of a bitch and turned away and started back for my house.

"Let me see," Vernon said. I knew he was a vet's assistant but I did not care. My poor cat was already dead.

"Get the hell away from me."

Then Merrill was out in the yard asking what was wrong

and I headed back across their yard, and I stepped across the fence—damn near fell over it—and I realized I was crying, holding poor dead Festus to my chest, bawling like a baby. I stood there in my yard, not knowing what to do for a minute or so. I heard Merrill call out to me but I just went around the house to the carport and laid Festus out on the hood of my car, and then I went into the house.

I dried my eyes on my sleeve. The house seemed dark, so I turned on some lights. It still seemed dark, so maybe that was me, maybe my eyes were messed up. I dried my tears on a towel. Then I went down the hall and into my office and got my shotgun out of the closet and took it out of the case. There was a box of number 4 shells on the shelf and I slipped two of them into the shotgun and pocketed a few others. My hands were shaking so badly I knocked the box over setting it back on the shelf and shells went rolling across the floor, but I didn't care. I went back down the hall and out the back door.

Vernon and Merrill were standing there, talking. The eagle was back on its pole, peering around and posing and acting like nothing happened. I crossed the yard, jacking the action just before I stepped across the fence. Vernon and Merrill were just looking at me. I aimed the shotgun at the eagle.

I warned Vernon and Merrill. "Stand back," I said.

"Now, Curtis, don't do that," Vernon said. "You don't want to do anything crazy."

I lowered the gun and glared at the son of a bitch.

"Crazy! *Crazy!* Your eagle killed my cat!"

"It's not the eagle's fault," Vernon said.

I just stared at him. I could not believe any sane man would say something like that.

"It's in the eagle's *nature*," Vernon said. "He's *supposed* to kill small animals."

I felt like I was going to start crying again. I said, "Well, it's in my nature to kill sons-of-bitches." I raised the shotgun again, and Vernon took a step toward me.

"Don't," he said.

"By God," I said, "I killed some Chinese fellas in Korea, and I doubt if they were any better men than you. So get out of my way."

I stood there with Vernon between me and the eagle, and I was so wrought up the barrel of the shotgun was shaking. Merrill was standing behind Vernon, behind the damn eagle, but she showed some sense and got out of the way, and went around to a corner of their yard and watched from there.

But that damn Vernon just stood there with his beard fluttering, standing between me and the eagle.

"C'mon, Curtis," he said. "You don't want to shoot. Besides, you can't shoot an eagle—you'd be committing a federal crime. You don't want to have to go to jail at your age. Do you?"

My arms were getting tired. The shotgun seemed so heavy. I was shaking. The barrel of the shotgun was wobbling around like Vernon's ugly beard. I knew I was going to cry again. I took a deep breath and steadied myself.

I said, "Step out of the way."

Reliction

When she took the time to look back on her life, Bonnie Chamberlain could see that she had always lived in a tortured world. Not just tortured through the normal heartbreaks of dying parents and stupid boyfriends and husbands—though, of course, like anyone else she had experienced those minor personal tortures—but tortured by time itself, vast, scary time, a span where mountains rose and eroded, oceans flooded and withdrew, where earthquakes and volcanoes went off, and strange creatures walked and flapped and swam.

She felt the pain of the world most of her life; when she was nine years old, some 45 million years after the last seas finally receded and the land that would become Texas emerged wet and steaming from the gunk, Bonnie found a fossil shark's tooth in the bed of a dry creek on her grandparent's farm. Long as her finger, black and gray and still sharp and scary-looking ages after being shed, the tooth was suddenly precious to her, a link to a hidden world—holding it in her hand, even as a child, she could almost feel the power, the mystery, the danger, the delight, the very life of the long-dead shark. Later she remembered looking up into the hills above the creek and being thrilled and scared to know that this had once been the floor of the ocean—and before that, a mountain range—and before that, and that, and that—*something* had always been there. She could feel the world spinning back, endlessly.

Thirty or so years later, hungover after a night of smoking pot and drinking wine, she had an idea: she could wear the past. She had boxes of fossils by this time: she'd spent many of her childhood weekends and summers searching for the remains of long dead animals—sharks and snails, oysters and ammonites—on the farm or even along the trash-filled and dangerous creek beds of Austin, where sometimes she would happen upon encampments of homeless men who would watch her hungrily.

By the time she was grown her collection was so large her husband complained about all the dusty rocks cluttering up their apartment. But, wearing the rocks. That would be something. So she began turning her favorite fossils into jewelry—wrapping strong gold-colored wires around the base of the shark teeth and tethering them to chokers filled out with blue or green glass beads and buff-colored bone spacers. They looked pretty good. Other people wanted them; she began to sell them and make a little money. She came up with other designs: earrings and charm bracelets made from fossil snail shells, and ashtrays she crafted from polished ancient oysters. But after a while Bonnie realized that her own fossils, the ones she found herself, were far too dear to sell, too precious, and she began buying her fossil shark teeth and snail and oyster shells from an Internet site based in Alabama.

Bonnie sold her jewelry at an open air craft market across the street from the university in Austin, a middle-aged white woman, hippie-ish and graying now but still fit and slender, sitting in the shade of an umbrella watching kids go by, occasionally selling a clunky snail-shell charm bracelet or ammonite amulet to a giggling girl. She was sitting at her table one noon when she spotted Travis, a would-be boyfriend, a would-be boyfriend she was already tiring of, making his way toward her through the crowd.

"Oh, it's you," Bonnie said. She sat up straight in her lawn chair and squinted at him. She asked, "What do you want?"

"I'm on lunch," Travis said. He worked in the bursar's office at the university, had met Bonnie online and they had gotten together a time or two for coffee. Bonnie was pretty much content to leave their relationship at that. Travis said, "I just thought I'd come see you—I thought maybe we could go get something to eat."

"But I'm working," Bonnie said.

"Well, yeah." Travis smiled nervously and made a show of admiring her jewelry. Then he looked up at her and smiled again. "Maybe I could bring you something?"

"I don't know." For Bonnie, the annoying thing about Travis was that he was well-meaning but boring. She didn't necessarily want a bad boy in her life—her ex-husband, Larry, had exhausted those desires—but she did want a man with a little spark to him, a little life, something. Travis lived with his mother, drank only a little, didn't smoke pot or do anything crazy or even eccentric, and he was pleased with the way Austin was getting bigger and bigger. He didn't mind traffic jams and he liked shopping at Wal-Mart and eating at chain restaurants. He had a very anxious sense of humor, as if he worried that laughter was a bad thing, and Bonnie could picture him sitting nervously in a car with his aged mother, driving slowly from one gruesome big-box retailer to another, caught in traffic, afraid to crack a joke or even gripe. Looking at him now standing nervously in the warm spring sunshine, Bonnie wondered why she even bothered talking to him. Romantic pickings were mighty slim, she thought. She said, "You stand there twitching like that, people'll think you're crazy. Somebody'll call the cops on you."

Travis picked up a trilobite from her table. "Did you find this one?"

"I bought it," Bonnie said. She pulled it from his hand and placed it back on the table. "It comes from Morocco—all the best trilobites come from Morocco anymore."

"Wow," Travis said, impressed. "All the way from Morocco. Just think."

A blonde girl who had been looking at a shark's tooth necklace stepped up to buy it. Bonnie smiled at the girl, noticing that Travis sort of wanted to check out the girl's ass but was also sort of afraid to. She shook her head. When the girl left with the necklace, Bonnie said, "Travis."

"Hey, you know, I just thought I'd say hello. I thought we could maybe get something to eat."

Resistance was useless. Bonnie sighed and sent Travis up the street to get cheeseburgers. She sat back in her chair, waiting, watching people, watching traffic, when she saw a battered black taxicab go down Guadalupe Street. The horn honked and the driver waved. Larry, her ex-husband. He drove by three, four, five times a day, and always honked. He was annoying, too.

★ ★ ★

Later, at home, Bonnie was sitting by the window working on bracelets, waiting for Larry to come take her to her other job, at a used bookstore, when she looked up to see Larry's cab pulling into the driveway. Bonnie lived in a garage apartment at the back of a fine older house in Tarrytown, and she knew the rich old lady lawyer who owned the house didn't like to see Larry's dented black taxi parked out front. But the old bitch was raising the rent and would probably price her out eventually, so who cared what she didn't like. Screw her. Bonnie heard Larry's heavy steps on the stairs and then he appeared at the door and let himself in.

"Damn," Larry said. Bonnie watched him look around: the walls were covered with skulls, cow skulls of unknown breed, mainly, though Bonnie did have one fine Longhorn spread on the wall over the door, and her prize, a massive, hollow-eyed, buffalo skull. There were two goat skulls on the kitchen table that she used for candle holders, three white-tailed deer shoulder mounts she'd bought at yard sales, dusty and shedding, and a mule deer hide on her bedroom door. Most of the skulls Bonnie had gotten after she had run Larry off; he stood looking at them now, bewildered. Her yellow cat, Bruce, walked over and rubbed against Larry's legs. Larry asked, "Aren't you ever gonna stop getting this shit?"

"No," Bonnie said. She tied off the shark tooth and frowned. Then she said, "So, what do you want?"

Larry took a step back, bumped into the door. Always clumsy. He asked, "To take you to work?"

"You sure you didn't come over here to give me a hard time?" Bonnie stood up and went into the tiny kitchen to get her purse and keys. She heard Larry mumble something like, "Oh, okay, no," but she didn't pay attention. She said, "Seems like all you want to do is give me a hard time. You drive down the street and honk at me—" Bonnie came back into the front room and saw Larry still standing by the door, looking uncomfortable. "*Honk* at me, scare all the customers."

"I'm just trying to be friendly," Larry said. He had always been a big man, but he had puffed up and put on some serious weight in the year and a half since she had finally broke with him, and the bloated layer of fat over his muscles made him somehow even more menacing. Bonnie knew he scared people—who would want to get in a cab with him? He looked crazy.

"You been drinking?" Bonnie asked.

"Naw," Larry said. His graying hair was tousled and there were big cloudy bags under his eyes. He smiled, "At least, not since I woke up."

"Out," Bonnie said. She pushed Larry out onto the landing and shut the door behind them. "Why do you go honk your horn every time you drive by? It's incredibly annoying."

Larry turned and started clumping down the stairs. "I figure maybe I can get some business that way," he said over his shoulder. "Get some attention. Maybe somebody needs a ride."

"The only people getting into your cab are drunk or retarded," Bonnie said. "Or desperate. I should know." Her own car was in the shop.

"There's desperate people all up and down that street,"

Larry said. "Heck, there's desperate people everywhere." Larry sounded sad. He had tried to make it in the cab business as an owner-operator, and at one time had owned five cabs, but he always had trouble finding reliable drivers, and then accidents left him with wrecked cars to fix and crazy, usurious loans to pay off. Finally, Yellow Cab canceled his contracts. This was about the same time as things were coming apart in their marriage. Larry was drinking a lot, and was always very angry, though he never argued with her, never even raised his voice. Instead he would glare for a bit when she nagged at him and then stomp out to a bar and pick a fight with some other poor drunk. He had size on his side and usually won his fights, except when he was fighting cops. Larry said he'd left Yellow Cab over money issues, but Bonnie always suspected he was lying, that it had probably been over his temper. Maybe he'd beaten up a passenger or something. At any rate, he was gone from Yellow and now leased a cab from East Side, the city's sleaziest, lowest-rent cab company.

Bonnie got into the front seat of the cab and was confronted with a collage of photos taped to the dashboard and airbag of the car—photos of *her*. Larry was in some of them, but most of them were of her, alone. Photos from the old days, young Bonnie—Jesus, she thought—wearing short fraying cut-offs and t-shirts, holding beers or cigarettes, smiling, happy.

"Larry, stop it."

"Stop what?" he asked.

"This!" Bonnie tapped on the laminated photo collage. She tapped again on a photo of her standing outside a music hall; there was a colorful mural behind her. "This is crazy! You're crazy."

"You remember that show?" Larry asked. "We saw The Replacements. That was a good night."

"Take these pictures and *burn* them."

"I still care about you," Larry said primly.

"Well, you shouldn't."

"What—"

"Not like this, at least," Bonnie said. "Jesus. You're just totally creepy. And those drunk assholes you pick up will be looking at these—Larry, take the pictures off!"

"C'mon," Larry said, smiling again. "Look, you were so hot back then."

"Larry—"

"I mean, you still are, but—"

"Just stop it," Bonnie said. "Get these things off of here."

"I still care about you," Larry said again. He sounded like an old woman.

Bonnie stared out the window, silently. The cab crossed the river, heading south, moving slowly in pace with the traffic. The air was heavy and still, and storm clouds were building to the west. After a moment Bonnie began peeling the pictures off the airbag. Larry frowned but didn't try to stop her. By the time he pulled the cab into the strip mall where Bonnie worked, she was holding the photos in her hand and was glaring at him.

"I'll let you keep these if you promise not to put them back on the car."

"Aw, baby," Larry smiled.

"Otherwise I'll tear 'em up!"

Larry put the cab in park and rested his head on the steering wheel. "Oh, okay," he sighed. He looked up and smiled at her again. "Bonnie, you're so damn hard on me."

"You try living with you," Bonnie said. She opened the glove compartment to put the photos away, and a plastic flask of something tumbled out. She said, "Jesus."

"Huh?" Larry asked. "What do you mean? I *do* live with me—and you don't."

It was too much. Larry was too much. Bonnie dropped the photos to the car seat and got out of the car. "I'll call your cell when I'm ready to go home," she said, and shut the door.

★ ★ ★

The fossil jewelry of course didn't provide a living, and so

Bonnie also had a part-time job working at a used bookstore on South Lamar. Twenty years earlier the building, a red-brick strip mall, had housed a dance club. Bonnie had gone there often with friends before she met Larry, and even after they started dating they had gone there a few times—Larry was too big and clumsy to dance but liked looking at all the girls. She hadn't seen any photos of the dance club on the dashboard of the cab, but there were probably some around, somewhere.

A young man—a boy, really, a part-time student at the community college—named Toby greeted her at the door when she came in.

"Hi," Toby said, slowly, when Bonnie walked in. *Hh-hh-iiiiiii.* He'd probably been out back smoking pot behind the dumpster. Toby worked with her most evenings, and he showed her lots of attention. He even tried ineptly to flirt with her, which Bonnie supposed was flattering though a waste of time for both of them. She wondered why he wasn't wasting his time hitting on the skinny little girl with the piercings who also worked at the store.

"Hey," Bonnie said. She glanced back outside and saw Larry's cab still parked in front of the store blocking traffic. He was sort of bent over—was he taping the photos back up? That fool. If he was, he was in trouble. He'd be better off taking a hit or two or three from the flask.

"We...got some books to...un*box*," Toby said.

"What?" Bonnie blinked and looked at Toby, and found him staring at her chest—maybe at the small trilobite amulet riding between her breasts, but probably not. He smiled toothily at her. Bonnie had once ot twice tried imagining Toby naked sometimes: scrawny shoulders, flat belly, muscular legs—he rode his bicycle everywhere. He had a pony-tail and a goatee and lively brown eyes and was in some ways totally revolting. Looking at him Bonnie was certain he had a skinny, crooked penis, though she was also pretty sure she didn't want to find out.

"Oh, good," Bonnie said. Unpacking and sorting books

gave her a chance to work alone. She headed for the back of the store.

★ ★ ★

While she worked, clouds built up and a thunderstorm rolled in from the west. She could see flashes of lightning and hear the patter of rain as the wind blew drops against the glass. When she took a break it was dark out, and sudden gusts blew sheets of rain and tumbled Styrofoam cups and paper food-wrappers across the parking until they lodged in a hedge. Larry's car was gone, of course: rain brought him business and money. Tonya, the girl with the piercings—eyebrow, lip, tongue, probably hidden areas—said, "I just love big storms!"

Toby said, "Yeah."

Tonya held the door open while Toby and Bonnie pushed carts of sale books back inside. Bonnie could smell the rain—smell dampness on the wind.

Toby said, "It's—exciting, huh?"

Bonnie shrugged. "I guess."

There was a crack of thunder and it began to rain harder. Tonya went back inside the store. Bonnie and Toby stood out of the rain, under the awning, and watched the storm. The walkway around the store was paved with flags of limestone, stone that was pitted with the shells of small ancient bivalves. The store, she thought, the dance club, the farm that was probably here before that, when Lamar Boulevard was the main road to Fredericksburg and points west, the grasslands that were here before that—and everything else that had stood here, or lived here. It made Bonnie sad, for once, the passing of time. Nothing to do about it, though.

Bonnie turned away from the wind and lit a cigarette. Toby pointed across the parking lot at a restaurant and bar, and said, "We ought to play pool sometime."

Thunder rolled and Bonnie didn't quite hear him. She asked, "What?"

"Play pool."

Through the rain Bonnie looked across the lot and saw two couples, two boys, two girls, playing pool. One of the boys shot carefully and stood up apparently smiling after a missed shot.

"Yeah," Bonnie said. "Right."

"Really," Toby said.

Bonnie smoked her cigarette and watched the rain. The pits in the limestone were filling with water blown in by the wind, and Bonnie flattened back against the windows of the store to stay dry.

After a while Toby asked, "Are you coming back in?"

Bonnie looked at him. "Why the hell are men always asking me what I'm gonna do?"

Toby took a step back. "Sorry," he said. After a moment he turned and went back into the store. Bonnie felt guilty: it wasn't the poor kid's fault that he was—a kid. Still, all the questions were a bit much. What did she know about what she was going to do—about anything? Of course, all her life she'd been asking various men what they wanted, and not a single one had ever been able to give her a satisfactory answer. Not really.

Bonnie didn't feel like going back inside to mess with the books. She stood on the limestone walkway smoking and watching the heavy rain, occasionally looking across at the bar to check on the kids playing pool. After its peak the storm tapered off quickly and blew on to the east. Bonnie lit another cigarette and walked around to the back of the building. Water was still dripping from the eaves and from the leaves of the live oaks, but the sky was clearing—in the upward-reflected lights of the city, she could see the shining clouds tearing apart and reforming as the wind pushed them east. Occasionally the bright spot of a star or planet would peep through the milky slashes and once she looked up to see the flashing strobes of an airliner making its approach to the airport before it was obscured.

At the bottom of the parking lot there were two large

concrete settling ponds, basins to catch and slow the runoff from heavy rains. The ponds were filling now, water and litter from the parking lots pouring in. Just as Bonnie turned to head back to the store, she saw something bobbing in the dark water, something—alive.

Bonnie stepped closer and looked down into the pond. The surface of the water was some three feet beneath the lip of the concrete rim and was covered with a skim of crud and trash, clots of leaves and sticks and an appalling number of Styrofoam food containers. But some sort of creature was swimming around in the water, too, and when it pushed between hamburger boxes and paddled into a shaft of light from a streetlamp she saw that it was a possum. She thought, poor possum. The possum paused, as if sensing Bonnie's thought, and looked up at her for a moment, bobbing amid the Styrofoam trash. Then it went back to swimming along the concrete walls of the holding pond. There was no way for it to get out, and the water in the holding ponds would often stand for days as it slowly drained back into the aquifer. The possum was doomed.

Bonnie stood up. There had to be a way to get the possum out of the water. She thought about calling Animal Control or Wildlife Rescue, but it might be the next day before they got out—too late for the tiring and bedraggled possum. It would drown. The dead possum would decay on the muddy bottom of the pond, buried by debris. Maybe at some point the pond would be scraped out and the dreck trucked off to a landfill somewhere—the body of the possum preserved, perhaps, in a bed of plastic coffee cups. No go, Bonnie thought. The future world would have to find its fossils somewhere else. She walked past the pond and along a chain-link fence, under a line of dripping trees, looking for a stick or something. Eventually she found a long strip of ¼ inch plywood, six or eight inches wide, maybe four feet long. She thought maybe she could sort of flip the possum out of the water.

Back at the tank Bonnie leaned over the concrete lip—it came up to about her knee—and reached down toward the possum with the board. The possum swam away from her, paddling briskly to the other side. Bonnie said, "Come back here."

The possum tried climbing the wall opposite from her, scratching at the concrete, bobbing amid the trash. Bonnie went around to the other side and tried herding the possum into the corner. Twice it ducked away from her, but the third time she pinned it and it wasn't able to swim away. It looked up past her and blinked. Bonnie said, "Hold still."

But as she tried to slide the possum up the wall, it jerked or something, and when Bonnie lunged after it she lost her balance and tumbled into the water. *Oh shit*, she thought—the water seemed to come at her very slowly, and then she was under it, and her head was up, and all she could think of was to get away from the goddamn possum. She lurched backwards, feet finding purchase on the muddy bottom, and then her head was above water. She slipped and sat back down with a tremendous splash.

"Fuck!"

Sitting down, the water was up to her chest or shoulders or chin—it was hard to tell with all the goddamn waves roiling back and forth—but she managed to scramble up, and the water was only about halfway up her thighs. Bonnie spat water and said, "Shit!"

The possum was back in the corner, trying to climb the wall. The strip of plywood was floating next to her. What the hell. Bonnie took the plywood and splashed over to the possum. It tried to swim back the other way, but she stopped it with the board and pushed again to the corner. "Hold still," she said again, and she managed to get the end of the plywood under the struggling possum and quickly flip it up and over the lip of the settling pond. She heard the possum hit the wet ground outside and scramble off into the soggy weeds. "Shit," Bonnie said again, and threw the strip of plywood into the water.

The lip of the pond was about at her chest level, and Bonnie managed to pull herself up and over it, and into the mud on the other side. When she stood up she was able see to the bar, see the people playing pool as if nothing had happened. They must have had a few drinks, for as she stood there, dripping, watching, three of the kids in a row missed shots and cheerfully danced back to the bar. Dancing—laughing. Oh, the kids. Dry, happy. Young. Lucky! Bonnie had a sudden dread of going home alone to her cat and the skulls.

Bonnie made her dripping way back up and around to the bookstore. Inside they were getting ready to close. Tonya was shelving some books, and Toby was standing at the cash register. Dry. Young. Bonnie went to the front and opened the door and went in. Toby looked up at her—shocked, Bonnie was happy to see, shocked, and concerned.

"What happened?" Toby blurted—shocked into almost normal sober speech. "You're all wet!"

Bonnie walked over to the younger man. The boy.

"You're going to have to buy me a drink after work," Bonnie said. She ran her hand through her hair and muddy water ran down her cheek. She noticed that her shirt was opened another button, and that her trilobite amulet was askew. She looked up to see Toby staring at her chest, and she smiled at him. Bonnie said, "Maybe three or four drinks. And then you can take me home."

Speed of Sound

Janet Flood was thinking once again about driving off into the sunset—about driving away and never coming back—when she heard a loud, rumbling bang. She looked up from the newspaper she was trying to read. The windows rattled but outside the sun was shining, and though she could see bushes moving in the heavy fall wind the world seemed very pleasant and normal.

"What was that?" her son asked.

"Sonic boom," Janet said. "It means a plane just broke the sound barrier."

Jay looked across the table at her. He had deep brown eyes and was puzzled.

"Hurry up and eat your cereal," Janet said. "It'll get all soggy."

"But what's the sound barrier?"

Janet put down the newspaper and lit a cigarette, and thought for a moment, looking out the window and thinking of airplanes. Her son watched her, waiting with his spoon in his hand.

"It's when a plane goes faster than the speed of sound," Janet said. "You know what that is?"

Jay shook his head.

"Okay, let's say that airplane came busting through the

wall just now"—Janet pointed with her cigarette at the wall just behind Jay—"and I yelled 'Get down, Jay!' But no matter how fast I yelled at you, the plane would still run you over, 'cause it would be going faster than my words."

Jay twisted around in his chair and looked at the wall, as if judging the likelihood of a jet bursting through it at any moment. Then he turned back to his cereal and began eating, every now and then looking up at his mother. He didn't say anything.

Janet looked back at the paper and tried to read. Her ex-husband, Steve, was the high school football coach, and his team had lost again. "We were just flat out beat," Steve was quoted as saying. Janet thought that even though half the football coaches in Texas said that line every week it still sounded particularly like Steve. He was the kind of man who treasured clichés the way other men treasured gold or silver. He even thought in them. Next week his team was playing De Leon. "De Leon has a fine squad this year," Steve said. "We're going to have to work hard to prepare for them." Steve was boring.

"So if the plane came through the wall, would it hit you?"

Janet looked up at Jay and frowned. "Well, you'd have your back to it when it came through, but I'd be able to see it coming, so maybe I could duck down out of the way."

"It'd be coming fast, right?"

"Real fast," Janet said. "But I'd still try to get under the table."

Jay nodded. "Me too."

Janet nodded back and mashed out her cigarette in the ashtray. She stood up and stretched, looking out the window again. White contrails lined the sky, fluffing out in the winds and dispersing. She wished she were on one of the planes: at the speed of sound, you could get a long way away, maybe before anyone even noticed you were gone.

"You better hurry so we can go see your dad," Janet said.

Jay hopped down off of his chair and ran back to his bedroom. Janet put on a jacket and gathered up her purse and a battered Rand McNally road atlas. Seven times in the last eight weeks she had dropped Jay off at Steve's, then set out on long drives out of town, driving eight or ten or twelve hours, thinking, thinking, stopping late for a motel room—twice sleeping in the front seat of her car—then turning back in the early morning and heading home. Each drive—to Dalhart, Clovis, Carlsbad, El Paso, Big Bend, Wichita, Little Rock—she saw as a dry run, practice for when she really left town for good.

Jay came back carrying a storybook for his father to read to him and a videotape of cartoons for them to watch. Janet stuck the book and the video into an overnight bag she'd already put together and helped Jay into his jacket, and then shooed him outside to the car, locking the door behind her.

They drove downtown and circled the town square—a Shelbyville square, Janet remembered from a Texas Geography class she'd taken when she was in college. College seemed a long time ago, but for some reason she could still tell the difference between a Shelbyville square and a Harrisburg square. Not that anybody else she knew ever seemed to give a damn. Many of the storefronts facing onto the square were vacant, the retail trade in the town having mostly relocated to a strip out on the highway centering around the Wal-Mart, but still the courthouse looked nice, surrounded by huge oaks, and the county historical society had restored and relocated a dog-trot cabin to one corner of the square for a museum.

Janet taught second grade at the elementary school, and her friends there knew that recently she had been gone almost every weekend. The ones who gave it some thought assumed she had a boyfriend—a married boyfriend, probably—in Ft. Worth or Dallas. Janet encouraged them to think so, smiling slyly when people asked about her weekends, knowing that when she finally left town for good, they really would have something to talk about.

"They had a band there last week," Jay said. He pointed at the front steps of the courthouse. "Dad took me."

"I know," Janet said. "He told me. Did you guys have fun?"

"Uh-huh," Jay nodded. "The band, they were like from the Army or something."

"Yeah, your dad said they were from Ft. Hood."

Janet circled the courthouse and headed east, out of town. Jay looked at her.

"This isn't the way to Dad's house."

"We're going to stop over and see Kevin first," Janet said. "Remember him?"

"He's the guy with all the junk."

"Yep, he sure is," Janet said. "He's got lots and lots of junk."

An anarchist's black flag was flying over Kevin's trailer, snapping in the wind, and a yellow tomcat sat on the hood of a rusting, long-dead Datsun pickup truck, watching them drive up. Weeds were growing from the bed of the truck, and they were bending in the wind, too, and the yellow tomcat's fur was ruffled. Janet got out of the car and looked to the sky, but the white contrails were gone, blown away. She walked up to the steps and banged on the door. After a few minutes she heard a faint "Come in" and opened the door—and then jumped back as a set of golf clubs fell at her.

"Jesus!" Janet caught the golf bag by its handle and set it back up. Six others—and clubs, and balls—were scattered across the floor in the midst of hundreds of magazines and books. Records and videotapes and compact discs and cassettes lined the walls, stacked as high as the windows. There was barely room to move around the trailer.

"Just set those up somewhere," Kevin said. He was sprawled out on the couch, a remote control box balanced on his gut. There were three televisions on a shelf at the foot of the couch—one was showing some sort of space movie, with robots and explosions and naked women, and the other two were showing football games.

Janet asked, "What's with all the golf clubs?"

"I'm trying to put together one really good set," Kevin

said. "It's not easy."

Janet made her way across the floor to the couch. Kevin moved his feet a little, and she sat down. She looked at a golf bag on the floor and saw a gunstock sticking out.

"You have a shotgun in your new set?"

"I saw some doves last time I was at the course." Kevin kept his eyes on a television—Janet couldn't tell which one he was watching.

Jay stood near the door, looking at his mother, then at the golf clubs. After a moment he crossed the room and looked at a computer that was half-buried under a stack of basketball magazines.

"Hit the return button, kid," Kevin said. "I got a submarine game on there that's pretty good. You can blow up the whole Soviet navy if you want."

"Don't touch anything," Janet said. "We won't be here very long."

"It's okay," Kevin said. "He won't break it."

Janet shrugged and looked at the TV with the movie on it. A naked woman zapped a guy with some sort of laser pistol.

"Did you hear that sonic boom this morning?" she asked.

"Yeah!" Jay said. "The sonic boom!"

"Huh-uh," Kevin said. He was staring at the televisions. "I didn't hear anything. Were we under attack?"

"It was just maneuvers or something, I guess."

"Those sonic booms," Jay said, "you know, if a plane came through the wall, it'd hit you."

"Yeah?" Kevin looked away from the TV, at Jay, thinking. "I remember when I was in Nam, and at night we used to sit up on the bunkers and watch Arc Light missions. The 52s were dropping bombs, you know, thirty or forty miles away, and you could still feel the ground shake where we were at. It was pretty impressive. I'd like to go back there someday and play golf."

"They used to service those planes at Bergstrom," Janet said. Janet had lived on several bases as a child, but had grown up mainly at Offut, near Omaha, and Bergstrom, outside of Austin. The B-52s had been a big part of her life, huge black planes, loud, spilling great dark clouds of exhaust, so big it was hard to believe they could fly. Then Bergstrom changed missions and the B-52s were gone, and the base supported a tactical reconnaissance wing that flew RF-4Cs, a plane her father had loved, a plane somehow even louder than the B-52. Her father would stand in the yard when he was home from work, barbecuing or mowing or whatever, and he'd look up at the Phantoms, grinning. "Little girl," he'd say, happy, "those there are the loudest aircraft in the Free World." But now her father was dead, of a heart attack, and Bergstrom had closed for budgetary reasons and then reopened as the municipal airport, and the Loudest Aircraft in the Free World were retired out west somewhere—Nevada or someplace—parked silently out in the desert where there wasn't anybody to look at them and grin.

"Your dad ever make it to Nam?" Kevin asked.

"He had a tour in Thailand," Janet said. "I was real little then. We stayed in Omaha."

"Thailand was pretty nice," Kevin said. "I'd like to go back there, too. There wasn't much in the way of golf but there were always lots of chicks."

They were silent, then, and Janet looked closer at the football games, realizing that one was a Super Bowl from the 1970s—Vikings and Raiders—and the other was an old college game, Miami and Boston College, the one where the quarterback threw the miracle pass.

"You don't like new football, huh?" Janet asked.

"I only watch games if they're classics, and then I watch 'em over and over again," Kevin said. He fished around under the cushions of the sofa and brought out a clear plastic vial and handed it to Janet.

"Thanks," Janet said. She glanced over at Jay and saw that he was hitting keys on the computer: a weird-looking Soviet helicopter was dropping torpedoes on his submarine. She cupped the vial in her hand and looked at it, smiling at the tiny clear-tan chunks of methamphetamine.

"That's the good stuff," Kevin said.

"How much do I owe you?"

Kevin shook his head. "Just a sample. Tell me what you think of it later."

"Okay, thanks." Janet closed her hand around the vial and rapped Kevin on the knee with her fist.

"Your husband should give some to the football team if he's serious about beating De Leon."

Janet smiled and rapped Kevin on the knee again. She thought about poor dull Steve and his coming week of preparation for De Leon. Maybe I should move, she thought. Go away before the big game just so I wouldn't have to hear about it. Even at the elementary school people talked about Steve and the high school team; several of her students had big brothers who were football players, and they always found time to brag about them during show and tell. It got old after a while.

"I'm thinking about moving," Janet said.

"You should move to Austin." Kevin didn't take his eyes on the televisions.

"I grew up in Austin. I know too many people there."

"You could go back to school, do some drugs, hang out."

Janet shrugged. "I already did all that."

Jay didn't know any of the commands for the submarine game and was getting frustrated. A Soviet cruiser was chasing him now, dropping depth charges. He couldn't get away. Finally his submarine broke up and sank to the bottom and he stared at the screen, frowning.

"We better go," Janet said. "I need to drop Jay off at his dad's."

"Take him some zip if you want," Kevin said.

"I don't think so." Janet stood up. "C'mon Jay, let's go."

"I want to try this again," Jay said.

"You'll just get sunk." Janet took Jay by the shoulder and aimed him toward the door. "Don't trip over the clubs."

"Listen," Kevin said, breaking away from the televisions

and looking up at her. "Next time drop the kid off first, then come over here."

Janet looked at him, arching an eyebrow. Kevin tugged at his shirttail, trying to cover up an erection—or maybe he was calling attention to it. Either way Janet thought he was silly, and she smiled. Kevin, in his way, was just as boring at Steve. The only times he left his trailer was to run to the all-night convenience store to get chocolate milk and cupcakes and magazines, or, more rarely, to go to Austin to meet his speed connection and then go shopping for more stuff. Despite his collection of golf clubs Janet doubted that he'd ever leave the trailer to go hit golf balls or even to shoot doves.

"Maybe I will," Janet said. "I'll call you next week." She thought, maybe.

Kevin looked back at the football games and shook his head.

Steve lived in one of the newer areas on the west side of town, near the high school, just off the road to Brownwood. He had a new wife, Karla, and a Dalmatian named Spot, and a fenced backyard for Spot to run around in, and a seventeen-thousand dollar bass boat he kept parked in the driveway—a *purple* bass boat. Janet hated the thing: Steve had bought it while they were still married, used it three times, and then parked it in their driveway, taking up her parking spot. Now the boat was occupying Karla's parking spot, though as far as Janet could tell, Karla didn't seem to care.

Jay ran over to play with Spot, who was jumping and twisting around behind the fence, and Janet walked up the driveway, past the absurd bass boat, through the weightroom the garage had been transformed into, and into Steve's kitchen.

"We're here!" Janet called. She piled Jay's overnight stuff on the kitchen table and looked around. Everything was spotless—the room was so clean it looked unused. "Hey! Anybody home?"

"What?" Steve's voice came from the living room, and Janet walked around the corner and found him standing in front of a green chalk board, diagramming football plays. A grainy video of a high school football game was playing soundlessly.

"We're here," Janet said again.

Steve glanced at her, then looked back at the board. "I'm thinking about De Leon," he said.

"Where's Karla?" Janet asked.

"I think she went out."

Janet was just as glad to have missed her. She always felt small and insignificant around Karla, who was a big, strapping blonde woman, the coach of the girls' basketball team. Up until the time she married Steve the small-town gossip had made Karla out to be a lesbian, and Janet still wondered if perhaps she and Steve didn't just get together to do relatively innocent things like lift weights and run.

Janet leaned against the door frame and watched Steve diagram plays. She said, "You know, I always wished those x's and o's stood for hugs and kisses."

Steve looked at her and blinked. "De Leon's got this fullback named Lichtenberg, and he's real good. Look." Steve took the remote and backed the video up, then fast-forwarded until he found the play he wanted. Some big kid carried the ball for a nice six-yard gain. "I don't know how the hell we're gonna stop him."

"Well, I don't know, either," Janet said.

"I'm thinking about having Arredondo blitz a lot," Steve said. He pointed at the chalkboard. "You know? Then have Miller cover the outside, and bring Heath and Johnson up—De Leon doesn't pass a lot. That way maybe we can throw off their rhythm. But still, if that Lichtenberg kid can get through the hole, you know, we're fucked."

"I imagine so," Janet said. She noticed that the light on his answering machine was flashing, and wondered who'd ever want to talk to Steve about anything.

Jay and Spot ran into the room, and Janet, who was allergic to dogs, backed away. Spot jumped up on her, anyway, and Jay dashed over to his father.

"Of course, if we can wait till Killer grows up we'll kick their ass," Steve said. He scooped up Jay and slung him over his shoulder. "Right, Killer?"

"We'll kick their ass!" Jay yelled. "We'll kick their ass!"

"Yeah!" Steve yelled.

Janet pushed the dog away, and stepped around Steve and looked at the back of her son's head. He was pounding on Steve's back.

"You do what your dad says, okay?"

"We'll kick their ass!"

"Okay, well, you do that." Janet kissed Jay behind his ear. "I'll be back to pick up you tomorrow evening." But the words caught in her throat: she wasn't sure if she was telling him the truth or not, and she had never consciously lied to her son before.

Steve, dull as he was, seemed to pick up on something in her attitude, and turned and looked at Janet closely. She had to lean back to avoid Jay's kicking feet.

"Where're you going to be going?" he asked.

"I thought I might drive down to San Antonio and see Mom." It was okay to lie to Steve about things.

"Oh," Steve said. "You want to take Jay? I bet your mom would like to see him."

Janet rolled her eyes. "We're just going to go shopping and stuff. Jay'll get tired out and cranky and be miserable. He'll have more fun with you, you know?"

"Yeah, I guess." Steve was still looking at her. Janet realized that he'd probably heard rumors about the married boyfriend in Ft. Worth. "Well, tell your mom I said hey."

"I'll do that." Janet patted Jay on his back. "See you guys."

Janet quickly turned and went back out through the kitchen and the weight room, past the bass boat to her car. She looked back at the house and could see in the front picture window, see Steve and Jay jumping around in front of the chalkboard, the head of the dog bobbing up occasionally as they all danced.

Janet drove on out to the highway and headed west. She stopped at the first gas station she came to and filled her tank at the self-service pump. Then she went on into the bathroom and locked the door behind her. She opened her purse and took out the vial of crank and keyed some up to her nose. It felt wonderful—her nose burned and her eyes watered, and a moment later there was the familiar bitter aftertaste in her throat. Very good. You couldn't get a whole lot of crank onto a key but it was enough—enough. She snorted up into her left nostril and then put the vial back into her purse and washed her face. Her nose was running, a little, and she wiped it on a tissue and stepped back outside. Janet saw Karla standing in line to pay for gas, and went around to the back of the store and got a six-pack of Pepsi and then stood behind her.

"Hey there," she said.

Karla turned around, her tight curls of blonde hair bouncing. "Oh, hi. I thought that was your car out there."

"Yeah, I just stopped off to get some gas and some sodas."

"Me too," Karla said.

"I just got through dropping Jay off at your place."

"Oh, good," Karla said. She looked out at the highway, uncomfortable, then back at Janet. "We always enjoy having him, you know."

"Yeah, well, he likes running around over there and all."

Janet's mind was buzzing with things she wanted to say but before she could decide on exactly what she should say, the line moved up and Karla was paying for her gasoline. Despite the cool wind Karla was only wearing shorts and a red tank top, and Janet watched the muscles in her broad shoulders work as she dropped her money on the counter and then picked up her change. Karla was scary. Janet was about to tell her so, when Karla turned and said "See ya!" and went on out the door. Janet stepped up to the clerk and paid for her gas and Pepsi. The clerk gave Janet her change and when she looked out the window she saw Karla driving away, off to the bass boat, the dog, the weightroom, Steve, her son.

Back in her car, Janet headed west toward Brownwood, then north toward Abilene. The morning winds had brought in some clouds and she headed into the gray, keeping her car just above the speed limit, happy to be alone on the road. She passed drab pastures with cattle, and a red-tailed hawk sitting on a fence post, and then there was movement off to the right—a B-1 bomber, Janet saw, a problem plane her father had had little respect for. They were stationed at Dyess, just up the road near Abilene. She watched the plane bank, apparently making a runway approach, and thought of her father. After he retired from the Air Force he had moved to San Antonio, and Janet had stayed in Austin to go to college. One weekend she drove down for a visit, and just north of New Braunfels the muffler had dropped off her car. She drove the rest of the way down in a tremendously noisy car, roaring and backfiring, knowing that she'd have to ask her parents for money to get it fixed, embarrassed when other drivers passed her, waving their arms and mouthing, "You're muffler's gone!" And then when she got to her parents' house her father came out to meet her, smiling, and he said, "I could hear you three blocks away. By God, you must be the loudest little girl in the Free World."

Five Things

For his thirtieth birthday, John Garza's employees gave him a "surprise party." Garza knew all about it well in advance, of course—he was a good manager, and kept up with what was going on in his group, even knowing about things that were supposed to be secret—but still it was nice, anyway: Mary Ellen brought a cake, and Suzanne a giant, heart-shaped cookie. Kris brought sodas, and someone else—Conrad, Garza thought—brought chips. There were three different cards that all the employees had signed. Some of the other managers came over and got together with his employees and they all sang "Happy Birthday" to him, and the employees in the other groups all looked up from their work and smiled. Garza was embarrassed but pleased: for the first time in a long time he felt appreciated. He gave the employees a half hour of administrative time to party around and have fun and relax before he sent them back to work.

Garza was cleaning off the printout table that they'd used for the party when his boss, Janet, came over to talk to him.

"Are you still thinking about resigning?" she asked. She sat on the edge of his desk and watched him closely.

"I don't know," Garza said. He sat back in his chair and looked up at Janet. "Maybe. I kind of want to, you know?"

"Yeah," Janet said, nodding. "Listen, I know you're not

happy right now. I don't know exactly what the deal is with you, but I know you're not happy."

She paused, as if expecting Garza to tell her what was going on.

But Garza only shrugged. He said, "Yeah."

Janet frowned. "So, you know, you have to do what's right for yourself." She pushed a cake crumb off Garza's desk to the floor and looked at him intently—Janet had very light eyes, light coffee brown, and the way she stared at him made Garza nervous. "I've always told my employees that they have to do what's right for themselves. You know? But remember, we're at peak season right now, and if you resign it's really going to mess us up."

"I know that," Garza said.

"I *know* you know that. I just wanted to say it out loud."

"Well," Garza said. "Okay."

★ ★ ★

The other managers took Garza out to Happy Hour after work.

"I wish I could quit," Celia said. Her group shared a node with Garza's. "But the kids are still in school, you know, and Fred wants to go back to graduate school. All of a sudden everybody's depending on *me* to pay the mortgage!"

"The ingrates," Garza said.

"Yeah," Celia said. "The ingrates."

Garza said, "It's tough out there."

"Yeah, life is very tough." Celia took a long sip of her margarita. "I have eleven years until retirement. That's a long time."

"Holy shit!" Garza said. Eleven years—it seemed like forever. Poor Celia. He thought for a moment. "I guess I've got—damn—*nineteen* years to go. *That's* a long time."

"That's a very long time," Celia agreed. "Nineteen years. I bet you won't be here that long."

"Probably not," Garza said.

"If I were you, I'd quit," Celia said. She glanced across the table at Janet, who was arguing with a waiter, then looked back at Garza and smiled. Her eyes glittered. "Right in the middle of peak season—quit. It'll mess everything up. Janet'll go crazy. The whole Section will go crazy! It'll give everyone something to talk about!"

★ ★ ★

When he came to work on his birthday, Garza found a little package in his mailbox. It looked and felt like a book, and was wrapped in a sheet of error printout, and HAPPY BIRTHDAY was written across it with a blue highlighter. He recognized the handwriting of his ex-girlfriend, Lynn. He went over to his desk and sat down and ripped the error printout away. Inside—no surprise—was a book, a self-help book called *Growth though Self-Criticism: A New Paradigm for Personal Development*, by some Ph.D. or other. Garza frowned: Lynn was evidently implying that he had faults. He took the book home and put it on a shelf in his apartment for a couple of days, but then, one evening, having nothing better to do, got it out and looked at it.

Though the "self-criticism" in the title reminded Garza vaguely of something he'd read about the old Chinese communists, the book itself was relatively straightforward. It was written by some psychologist who gave case histories of patients who'd taken control of their lives by keeping a diary or journal. And though the case-history people seemed to be far more messed up than he felt he was, Garza was nonetheless intrigued. Maybe a diary could help him get a handle on things. For several months—since the beginning of the tax season, back in January—Garza had felt that he was drifting. He had come to hate working in Data Conversion, and he wanted out. He was only a temporary manager, and at the end of the season in June he would go back to his permanent job as the Section clerk-typist. Clerk-typist! What a job title! Four years of college at the big university, a degree in history, all for a lousy job as an IRS clerk-typist. Even some of the other managers, his friends, would look at him at times and say, "What the hell are you *doing* here?" Garza didn't know. His friends from college were out of law school now, or out of grad school, or out working for corporations and making good money, and Garza was stuck doing quality review on tax returns and writing up his employees for returning late from breaks. And he had turned thirty. That made a difference, too.

After reading four chapters of the book he sat down at his computer and wrote.

> Nancy the Branch Analyst came by my desk and asked what it was like being thirty—she's 28 or something like that and she said she wanted to know. I said it made me realize that my dick would never be as big as my Dad's. She's some sort of Christian or something and got embarrassed and walked away. Probably bring me up on sexual harassment charges now. I hope so.

Garza smiled. Embarrassing snotty Nancy was fun but it didn't really have anything to do with anything else.

> I am trapped at the fucking IRS! I don't really want to quit—but maybe Janet wants to get rid of me—I need the money. My poor employees—Janet says she'll send most of them over to Cynthia's group if I go. Cynthia sucks. What an asshole.

Garza thought for a moment. He was verging on the incoherent.

> Maybe if I can get some kind of life

going on outside the fucking IRS everything will be all right. Maybe.

He went to the kitchen and got a beer and went back to his desk. He opened the beer and read over what he'd written. No good.

But I don't even want to mention the IRS in this journal—I hate that fucking place! I just want to write about other stuff.

But *what* other stuff? Garza was suddenly depressed. There really wasn't anything in his life outside the IRS—everything, it seemed, was tied up there somehow. He played on the Section's softball team, he went to IRS parties, and his last three girlfriends had worked for the IRS. He had been to four IRS weddings and an IRS funeral. When he went to bars on the weekends he hung around with IRS people. When he went bowling he bowled with IRS people. The only person he had regular contact with who didn't work at the IRS was the little Nigerian guy who worked at the convenience store across the street from his apartment—and he'd told Garza that he planned to apply for a job at the IRS as soon as his citizenship papers came through.

It was a problem. He didn't want to write about work—he had arrived at a point where he dreaded the very thought of the IRS, almost in the same way a damn tax cheat would—but there didn't seem to be anything else in his life, anything at all, at least nothing worth putting in a journal.

He went back and read the journal book. It said that there were different kinds of diaries and journals, and one kind had nothing but lists of things. Garza—a bureaucrat at heart despite his weariness of the IRS—could appreciate the idea of a list.

So what I'll do is I'll just make a list of things I see—nothing to do with the IRS, nothing. Five things a day.

Garza thought for a moment. Five things suddenly seemed like a lot.

1. Pregnant hooker in a red tube top standing outside feed store on Congress Avenue waving at traffic.
2. Walking to the bank, passing by the Montessori School, a little bcy picks up a little girl and body slams her like on pro wrestling. The little girl cries but no one but me notices.
3. Stray cat with infected eye.
4. Girl with huge bosom bouncing down the jogging trail.

Garza read over his list and smiled. Jesus, he thought, maybe I am depressed. I'll put in number five tomorrow.

★ ★ ★

At work Garza's desk was right in front of the coffee pot, and over the course of the shift most of the coffee-drinking managers would come by at one time or another. Lynn was a big coffee drinker and whenever she came by she'd say "Hi," and Garza's chest would tighten and he'd look away. Lynn would look away, too. Since their big argument back in February they hadn't said much to one another.

But after Garza began his diary—his list—he waited for Lynn to come by his desk.

"Hi," Lynn said. She looked away and bent over the coffee pot.

"So what's the deal with the book?" Garza asked. "You think I have problems or something?"

Lynn stood up and sipped at her coffee, looking at him over the rim of her mug.

"I sort of hoped you wouldn't take it like that," she finally said. She glanced over and smiled at Celia—Celia was watching them closely, an eyebrow raised—and looked back at Garza.

"I don't know how I'm supposed to take it." Garza slouched down in his chair and scratched his chin. "You give me this book about personal growth—you think I need to grow?"

"I think everybody around this damn place needs to grow," Lynn said. She turned and walked away.

Garza spun his chair around and looked blankly at the Time and Attendance sheet on his desk. He just stared at the numbers for a minute.

"You okay?" Celia asked.

Garza looked up, suddenly aware of the 500 or so people working around him in the big room. He looked over at Celia and said, "Let's go to lunch and have a drink or five."

1. Kid running to get on a city bus but the bus leaves without him.
2. Broken glass from a car wreck at the intersection of Barton Springs and Lamar.
3. Two guys fighting to get on a pickup truck at the day labor pool.

"You need to snap out of this," Celia said. "Look at me: I'm a Mexican—I don't get depressed, I get pissed."

Garza smiled. "I'm Mexican, too," he said.

"I'm starting to wonder," Celia said. "You don't even speak Spanish. You can't even talk to your own grandmother."

"Well." Garza looked away. People had been giving him a hard time about that for years, Celia especially, ever since the time they'd been sitting around the happy hour patio and a butterfly had fluttered past and he had called it a paloma instead of a mariposa. She couldn't get over it. Garza didn't think it was his fault, though: No one ever spoke Spanish around the house when he was growing up, and in college he'd taken German as his foreign language. The fact that he could tell die Taube from der Schmetterling he kept to himself; if he told Celia, she'd probably just laugh at him.

"And how come you're depressed all the time?" Celia asked. "How come you're not pissed?"

"I get pissed all the time." Garza tilted his chair back from the table. "You have no idea how pissed I get."

"Well—right. Sure. So how come I never see you get pissed at Janet? So how come I never see you get pissed at Lynn?"

"I don't want to get pissed at Janet," Garza said. "I like Janet—she's a good boss. You know that. She leaves us alone."

"Yeah," Celia agreed. "She's a good boss. But you still ought to get pissed at her sometime, anyway, so she doesn't take you for granted. Same thing with Lynn."

Garza smiled at Celia. "I don't think either of those women take me for granted."

"That's what you think," Celia said. "How come you didn't get an award when you worked on the task force? Because they took you for granted—what else could they do? You always showed up on time, you always worked hard, you never complained—"

"So they took me for granted."

"So they took you for granted." Celia took a long sip of her margarita. She was enjoying this. "Nobody takes me for granted."

Garza knew that was true. Celia's instigation of the latest memo war proved that she should not be taken lightly. The day shift managers shared desks with the night shift managers, and there was always some tension between the shifts over who controlled what aspect of a desk. Back at the beginning of the season Celia had gotten angry about having to look at a photograph of her night shift counterpart's kids, which the night shift manager had propped up in a prominent place. They were ugly kids, Garza agreed, but he probably would not have complained about it, ever, and would have covered up the kids and used the picture frame for a document holder or something and then gone on about his business. But Celia complained to Janet, and kept on complaining until Janet carried the complaint to the Section Chief, who forwarded it to the Night Shift Section Chief, setting off a six-week memo war that ended only when the Branch Chief decided, Solomon-like, that all managers should clean off their desks at night and lock up all personal effects, like photographs of ugly children. Celia was pleased with her victory.

"And it's the same thing with Lynn," she said. "You're always there moping around, so she goes ahead and takes you for granted. You need to snap out of it."

"I need to snap out of it," Garza repeated. He thought about that and nodded.

1. Man fixing flat tire. Boy watching.
2. Mailman squirting angry dog with something. Mace?

Garza walked up the ramp onto the production floor. Lynn's desk was the nearest to the ramp, and when he came up the ramp they went through a process similar to the one they used when Lynn came over to the coffee pot: they said "Hello" and then looked away.

But now Garza marched directly over to Lynn's desk. She looked up from her terminal at him wide-eyed—frightened. It had never occurred to Garza before that Lynn might be frightened of him.

"Listen," Garza said. He spoke quietly, so that Lynn's employees could not hear, but distinctly. "I'm really tired of what's going on between us here. You know?"

"Yeah—but can't we talk about this later?" Lynn was visibly nervous. She glanced at her employees to see if they were watching her—some were—and then back at Garza.

"Huh-uh. I just want to say that I'm sick of this situation."

Lynn's eyes filled with tears and she looked away. "You must hate me so much."

"Hate—shit, the problem is the exact opposite of that. I don't hate you at all. But I *do* think you're an extremely destructive person. I think you're the one that needs the goddamn self-help book."

Before Lynn could say anything Garza turned and walked off, heading around the big bank of computers and up the far side of the room. He passed Angie's unit, and Steve's, and when he came past Celia's desk he tapped her on the shoulder. She was listening to her IPod and doing quality review and looked up, startled.

"Watch this," Garza said.

Celia pulled off her headphones and watched Garza.

He went past his own desk and over to Janet's. She was working on her Time and Attendance roster.

"Hey, there," Garza said.

Janet looked up. "Hey, John. What's up?"

"I finally decided to quit," Garza said. "I'll give you my official two-week notice tomorrow."

Garza turned around and went back to his desk.

"Hey, dude, come back here!" Janet said loudly. She put down the Time and Attendance sheet and stood up, her hands on her hips. "We going to need to talk about this, you know?"

```
1. Gunky water drains out of the dumpster
   when the truck comes to empty it
```

Garza had a hard time coming up with five things—only rarely could he fill his self-assigned quota of observations. There just didn't seem to be anything out there worth seeing. He wondered what he would do for fun after he quit the IRS.

```
2. The little Nigerian guy was cold
   because of the air conditioning in
   the store.
```

That was a really sad number two. He erased the line and tried to think of something else. He stared at the screen for another few minutes, his mind empty, then shut the computer off and went to bed.

★ ★ ★

Garza had barely unlocked his desk the next morning at work when he was summoned to the Section office. The Section secretary looked nervous and showed him in to the Section Chief, Lorraine Warton. Lorraine was a big black woman with a wide, flat nose and wild streaks of gray through her hair. Janet was sitting next to her looking small and mousy and quiet.

"What's this I hear about you wanting to quit?" Lorraine asked.

"I think I've got to," Garza said.

"Got to," Lorraine repeated flatly. "*Got* to?"

"Uh-huh."

"You know we're at peak right now."

"I know that," Garza said.

"He knows that," Janet said. "I made sure he knows that."

Lorraine ignored Janet, staring hard at Garza. "So if you *know* that, then why you want to quit? Huh? You don't remember that when you signed on as a manager you agreed to be responsible for your employees? You don't remember that you agreed to give quality service to the taxpayers?"

Garza tried not to smile. The only time anyone around the IRS mentioned the taxpayers was when they were trying to get one-up on someone else.

Garza said, "Oh, fuck the taxpayers."

Janet's eyes bulged out of her head and she looked away, trying not to laugh. Garza focused on the calendar on the wall behind Lorraine. Two more weeks, he thought.

"What!" Lorraine yelled. She slammed her big hand on her desk. "What!"

"I said, *fuck* the taxpayers," Garza repeated, louder. "They'll get their refunds just fine without me."

Lorraine stared at Garza for a moment. Then she looked at Janet.

"Did you hear what he said?"

Janet still looked like she was going to laugh but she managed a nod. "Uh-huh."

"What kind of unit are you running over there?"

Janet shrugged. "—I don't know."

"You don't know. You don't know." Lorraine looked at the top of her desk for a moment. She said, "Shit."

Garza was sorry he'd gotten Janet in trouble. He said, "Things are going smooth. You don't need me around here."

Lorraine looked up at him. "What do you know about it?"

Garza shrugged. "Not much, I guess."

Lorraine slapped her big hand on the desk again. "Pam!" she yelled.

The Section secretary stuck her head in the room.

"Why don't you start cutting the resignation papers on Mr. Garza."

Garza went back to his desk and sat down. Celia swung her chair around and looked at him, smiling.

"So how'd it go? We could hear Lorraine yelling all the way over here."

Garza grinned. "Aw, man, she went nuts."

One of Garza's employees, Mary Ellen, got up from her terminal and came over. She dropped a 1040 on his desk and pointed to the address.

"This guy's handwriting sucks," she said. "What's the name of that city?"

Garza bent over the document and squinted. "Dumas," he said. "It's way up in the panhandle, past Amarillo."

Mary Ellen looked at the document. "Huh." She trailed one hand along the top of his desk.

"Anything else you want?"

Mary Ellen said, "Yeah, are you really gonna quit?"

"Probably."

"So what's going to happen to us?" She waved her hand

at the other employees. Several of them were watching.

Garza sat back in his chair. "Some of you will go to Celia, some to Cynthia, some to Pete."

"We don't want to go anywhere else," Mary Ellen said. "We want to stay with you."

"You're gonna have to quit, then, huh?"

"You are so *incredibly* selfish," Mary Ellen said. She turned and headed back to her terminal. "You don't think about anybody but yourself."

1. Fog in the morning on way to XXX (that awful goddamn place that I'm not going to mention in this diary). Car headlights looked like fuzzy yellow balls.
2. Grocery store cart rolling across parking lot, smashing into a car. Fat woman running after it but too late.

Garza could not think of anything else. He picked up the phone and dialed Lynn's number. She answered on the second ring.

"Hey there," Garza said. "What're you doing?"

"John?"

"Yeah." Garza had the TV on mute, and rolled through the channels until he came to MTV. Someone was chasing a dwarf with a baseball bat. "I was wondering what you were doing."

"I'm correcting timesheets," Lynn said.

Garza looked at his own desk: there was a huge pile of work he had brought home for the weekend, including a stack of his employee's timesheets that had to be corrected.

"I suppose I should be working on mine," he said.

"Yeah, you should, unless you want them to fall out." Garza could hear Lynn light a cigarette—the click of the lighter, inhale, exhale. "Listen, why are you calling me?"

"I just wanted to know what you're doing."

"You're getting really weird, John."

"It's that book you gave me," Garza said. "It's causing me to fucking grow."

```
3. High school kids all dressed the same
   in black, one with a can of spray
   paint.
```

★ ★ ★

The next day Lorraine passed Garza in the hallway and she averted her eyes, not willing to look at him, gazing up at the ceiling; but later she made one of her rare appearances on the production floor, paying special attention to Garza's work area, pawing through the big carts of tax returns parked next to his desk and inspecting his paperwork very closely.

"Hey, I'm on top of everything," Garza said. "Everything's going out on cycle."

Lorraine put the clipboard back on the cart, then looked out at Garza's employees. They were all trying to keep one eye on Lorraine and the other on their computer screens, and they all seemed to be typing very slowly. Lorraine shook her head and looked at Garza.

"Do you know how much paperwork I'm gonna have to cut to transfer all your people to different groups?"

"Yeah," Garza said. Of course, he knew, Pam the secretary would cut all the paperwork; all Lorraine had to do was sign her name.

Lorraine loomed over his desk. "Listen, little boy, if you do leave, I don't ever want you coming back here to my Section. And if you change your mind and stay, I don't want you around my Section, either. Understood?"

Garza shrugged. "Sure," he said. He was a little hurt, though. He'd been Lorraine's clerk for three years and had kept her out of trouble plenty of times. And he hadn't even gotten an award for being on the task force.

"Okay, then." Lorraine rumbled off. Garza looked over at Celia, who was grinning at him. Mary Ellen came over and dropped a tax return onto his desk, her finger—deep red nail polish on it—tapping on the city line.

"Goldthwaite," Garza said. "With a 'th.' It's out on 183, up toward Brownwood."

"It's on the other side of Lometa," Celia said from her desk.

"Yeah," Garza repeated, "it's on the other side of Lometa."

Mary Ellen was looking past Garza, her eyes glittering with angry tears. Garza turned and saw that she was looking at Lorraine.

"That bitch," Mary Ellen said. "I can't believe she talked to you like that in front of everyone."

"She's just mad at me."

"She's a bitch." Mary Ellen snatched the return from Garza's desk and went back to her terminal. She sat down and looked back at Garza. "I'd kick her ass, man."

"Fred's sister lives in Abilene," Celia said. "We go through Goldthwaite every time we go out there."

"Nice, old-fashioned courthouse in Goldthwaite," Garza said.

"Very nice."

Garza looked over at Mary Ellen, who was wiping tears off her cheeks with a tissue while typing one-handed, blinking at the tax return in front of her.

1. Pickup truck weaving across traffic, and when I pass it I see two men in the front, fighting.

★ ★ ★

At one point in their relationship Garza had asked Lynn for a photo of herself, and she had handed over an enormous 14 by 24 print that one of her former boyfriends had made. It was a nice shot, but Garza had always wondered what the hell he was supposed to do with it. Even before they had broken up Garza couldn't imagine putting it on his wall—Lynn, bigger than life, a cigarette dangling from her lips, looking out at him all moody and sultry, like some French movie star. It was too good a photo to throw away, but Garza certainly didn't want it around any more. He dialed Lynn's number.

"Hey there."

There was a pause. "What do you want now?"

Garza looked at his desk. The huge photo was spread out across it, and his computer was open to the journal document. He needed three more things.

"I was wondering what you wanted me to do with that picture you gave me."

"I don't care," Lynn said.

"You don't want it back?"

"I don't care," Lynn said again. "Throw it away or something. Give it to Goodwill."

"Well, okay." Garza figured he'd stick it in a drawer somewhere.

"I heard you're really quitting," Lynn said. She paused, and Garza did not know what to say. "You must really hate me so fucking much."

```
2. Homeless man playing with a happy
   black dog in front of the Humane
   Society building.
```

★ ★ ★

Garza's desk phone rang, and he picked it up.

"Data Conversion, this is John."

"Get over here." It was Janet. Garza looked across to her desk; Janet was looking back at him, the phone to her ear. "Now." She hung up.

Garza went over and sat at her desk. "What's up?"

"I've got a bunch of stuff for you to sign," Janet said. She pushed a pile of paper toward him, a standard resignation packet: a Form 52, an Application for Refund of Retirement Deductions, a Form 2019, a Form SWR 272, and a Current/Former Spouse's Notification of Application for Retirement Deductions.

"Cool," Garza said. He had cut dozens of employee resignations as a clerk and a manager, and he went to work on his own, signing in the correct spaces, and pushing the Current/Former Spouse's Notification of Application for Retirement Deductions back to Janet, unsigned.

"I have no current or former spouse," he said.

Janet didn't say anything. She shoved the Current/Former Spouse Notification form under the Application Form, and put them both under the SWR 27, with the 2019 on top.

Garza stared at the Form 52. He was supposed to state his reason for resigning and sign it. He tried to think of a good reason for resigning and couldn't come up with anything very professional-sounding. Still, he had to have something. After a moment he wrote:

1. Want to go to grad school.
2. Want to go fishing.
3. Very dissatisfied. No awards.

"All done," Garza said. He slouched down in the chair. "As of tomorrow I'm out of here."

Janet was looking at his 52. "Fishing," she said flatly.

"Hey, spring's the best time of the year to go fishing, and every spring I'm cooped up in here doing the nation's business." In truth, Garza hated fishing; he just thought that mentioning it would piss Lorraine off even more.

"What're you going to do for money when you're going to grad school?" Janet asked.

Garza shrugged. He hadn't really thought of that. "Maybe I can get a fellowship or something."

"You're going to be on welfare," Janet said. "You're going to be a bum." She looked over the papers one more time, and sighed. "Okay, I want you to have all your paperwork—all your timesheets, even—completed by end of shift. Everything."

"Okay," Garza said.

Janet went through the resignation packet a third time, staring at the reasons for resignation given on his Form 52. She shook her head, like she couldn't get over it.

"John, you don't get awards for doing your job, you get awards for exceeding your job expectations. You know that. I've heard you tell your own employees that."

"I think Lorraine should give me an award for the task force," Garza said. "I did all the work."

"I just think you're lazy," Janet said. She put the 2019 on top of the 52, still shaking her head. "You're a bum. You just don't want to work anymore."

Garza looked at Janet. She was a small woman, compact and dark, with those strange light eyes. They had started out at the IRS at the same time, as rookie transcribers entering Windfall Profit Taxes, and when the WPT was repealed they moved on to 1040s and 1040-As, working in the same production unit that first confusing year, a bad year under a bad manager, a bad year that they both agreed later had made them good managers. Garza liked working for Janet, and he knew now that he was going to miss her.

"I just don't want to work *here*," he said. "It's got nothing to do with you, though."

Janet ignored that; she was not very sentimental. "Look at your pal Celia—" Janet pointed over at Celia, who was doing quality review but trying to keep an eye on the two of them. "She *likes* to work. She works *hard*."

Garza shrugged. "She's a Mexican."

"So are you!" Janet lowered her voice. "Except you're supposed to say *Hispanic*. We had a memo on that a couple weeks ago from the Director's Office. Didn't you read it?"

```
1. Woman next door takes out trash.
```

★ ★ ★

Garza looked across the room at the pile of paperwork—the damn timesheets—and thought about calling Lynn one last time, but decided not to. He needed to make his diary entry—five lousy things, and he couldn't even think of two or three—and then get to work on the timesheets. Get them worked up tonight, and the 3926s for Quality Review, and then he could walk out the IRS door tomorrow a free man.

1. Woman on roller blades walking—skating?—her Dalmatian. Big dog, pretty woman.
2. Baby with dirty face at the grocery store, crying. No one pays attention except me.

★ ★ ★

On his last day Garza's employees had wanted to give him a going away party but Lorraine, still angry, had refused to allow them any administrative leave and so they sat, working slowly, slowly. In the two weeks since he had decided to quit, the group's productivity had declined almost fifty percent. Garza didn't really care about productivity anymore, but it did bother him that his group's morale was so low. Mary Ellen cried openly for a time, and none of the other transcribers looked happy. None of them knew what manager they would be working for next week; Lorraine had delayed processing the transfer papers so that Garza would not be able to announce their new groups, and they would not find out until they came in for work on Monday. In the afternoon Lorraine peeked out of her office every now and then, looking at Garza's group to see if he was still there, and checking to see if Pam the Section secretary had completed work on transferring Garza's employees to their new groups. When Garza caught her looking his way Lorraine would just turn and go back to her desk. He felt sorry for her: Lorraine would be stuck at the IRS forever. They'd have to take her out in a box.

Garza worked as steadily as he could—there were interruptions, people stopping by his desk to say good-bye—and got his quality review transmittals ready and dropped them on Janet's desk.

"Okay," Janet said. "Are you going to have your timesheets done?"

"I don't know," Garza said. "I hope so." Janet stared at him until he got nervous and looked away. "Well, maybe the production volume will be a little off."

"A little off," Janet repeated. She shook her head. "Just put them on my desk at four-thirty, and I'll finish them."

Garza cleaned out his desk. He gave Celia his calculator with the big keys, he gave Angie his quality review notebook with the highlighted error codes, he gave each of his fourteen employees a U.S. Government mechanical pencil from a box of pencils he had hoarded years earlier, he gave Cynthia his good hole-puncher even though he didn't like her, and he went over and gave Lynn his stapler, dropping it on her desk as she worked.

"Thanks," she said. She took the stapler and tried it out on the document she was reviewing. "Hey, it works."

"I've always known you've had an eye on my stapler."

Lynn said, "I hear they're taking you out for happy hour after work."

"Yeah, I guess," Garza said. "You coming?"

Lynn just shrugged and Garza went back to his desk. He made three trips out to his car, carrying boxes of junk, and when he came back for the last time his employees were putting up the work and getting ready to knock off for the day. Garza felt unexpectedly moved: they were a good bunch of kids. Their error rates were a bit high, but that was as much his fault as theirs.

"Hey, everybody? Hey!" Everyone looked at him. Garza said, "Thanks a lot for all your work and stuff."

"Shut up, John," Celia said. "We don't want to hear any speeches."

"You're abandoning us," Mary Ellen said.

Garza sat at his desk. Celia was stacking her paperwork, almost done for the day—for the week. Garza wasn't coming back but he still had lots to do, a huge pile of paper that had to be dealt with.

"And you're the guy who wanted an award." Janet stood behind him. Garza swiveled his chair around and just shrugged and grinned at her. "I guess I'll finish everything off," Janet said. "C'mon, let me walk you to the door."

Celia was standing there, a bundle of paper clutched to her chest. Garza put on his jacket.

"I'm parked out back," he said.

Janet frowned. "You would be parked all the way out back on the other side of the building, and then leave me all your work to do."

Garza glanced around the floor one more time—there was Lynn dropping off her transmittals, and Lorraine glaring at him. Employees heading for the front door. He turned and the three of them walked off the floor and up the long hallway past Error Correction, past the nurse's station, past Batching and Numbering, past Receipt and Control, to the back door. They went out and stood on the back steps, a flow of employees getting off work parting to go around them, and Garza took off his badge and handed it to Janet. She took it, and gave him a hug.

"I know you hate this," Janet said. "You're going to miss this place."

Garza pulled away from her, looking past her across the vast parking lot to the rush-hour traffic backed-up on the highway, to the little kids playing at the day care center, at a truck unloading at the warehouse, at a guy changing the sign at the movie theater across the street, at a stray cat running from under a parked car to hide in a culvert.

He said, "I don't know yet."

About this Edition

I've made a few changes to the text of this edition—most notably, to a couple of the story titles.

The story formerly called "Brindled Pit Bull" is now titled "Top Dog in the Kill Chain." Which was actually the original title—something I had forgotten, until one day while packing for a move I came across the notebook where the story was started. "Brindled Pit Bull" is a decent title, but not as good as "Top Dog in the Kill Chain." I don't remember why I changed it, but now I'm changing it back.

"Bad Guts" was originally titled..."Bad Guts." I changed the title to "Chitterlins" when I revised the story and included it in my MA thesis. Then when I revised the story again for inclusion in the first edition of *Long Time Ago Good*, I changed it to "~~GUTS~~ ☹" Which was a little bit too much change. The title originally came from a writing prompt I got from novelist W.P. Kinsella at a summer workshop: "Write a story called 'Bad Guts.'" And so this is it, finally.

LMW

About Lowell Mick White

Lowell Mick White is the author of three books: *That Demon Life* and *Professed*, novels, and *Long Time Ago Good*, a story collection. His work has been published in many literary journals, including *Callaloo*, *Iron Horse Literary Review*, and *Short Story*. A winner of the Dobie-Paisano Fellowship, awarded by the University of Texas at Austin and the Texas Institute of Letters, White has been a lecturer at Texas A&M University and has been the National Endowment for the Arts Artist-in-Residence at the federal prison in Bryan, Texas. He was recently inducted into the Texas Institute of Letters.

White can be contacted at www.lowellmickwhite.com

www.ingramcontent.com/pod-product-compliance
Lightning Source LLC
Chambersburg PA
CBHW021021120726
47905CB00009B/3123

* 9 7 8 0 9 9 0 8 6 3 2 8 1 *